Rough Trail to the Pulpit

C. C. Rouse

D1740258

Pacific Press Publishing Association
Mountain View, California
Oshawa, Ontario

Cover art by Sue Rother

Library of Congress Cataloging in Publication Data

Rouse, C. C.
  Rough trail to the pulpit

  1. Rouse, C. C. 2. Seventh-Day Adventists—United States—
Biography. I Title.
BX6193.R68A37   286.7'3   [B]   81-2672
ISBN 0-8163-0434-3   AACR2

DEDICATION

MY PRAYER

Dear Father of mankind, I pray
  For strength and wisdom day by day
To walk the straight and narrow way—
  In fatherly love Thy life display,
So three small boys won't go astray.

Help me in all I say and do
  To be sincere, upright, and true.
Each morning may Thy Spirit imbue
  To teach my charges Thine honor due,
So three small boys will love Thee too.

In the rolls of prophecy we're told
  Of the city of God, with the streets of gold;
With mansions there for the saints' abode.
  May three small boys find now the road
That leads at last to joy untold.

So in the earth made new I'll meet
  My three small boys at Jesus' feet—
With Mother, too, I'd surely greet
  And know the joy of life complete.
Ah, what a reunion (a thought so sweet).
                                    Amen.

Life With a Horse Trader

Sometimes trading a team of horses can upset a family more than almost anything else. Especially if the father is a horse trader by trade and is married to another horse lover who gives birth to sons also destined to be horse lovers.

Such was the case with the Rouse family a long generation ago in the Gallatin Valley of Montana.

Clifford Rouse and his older brother Floyd arrived home from school one spring day to find their mother in tears. She was not one to cry easily; and Cliff, who entered the kitchen while Floyd headed for the barn, was alarmed.

"What's the matter, Mama?" he asked softly. "Is something wrong?"

She brushed away wisps of blond hair that strayed down to mingle with her tears.

"Oh, no, she said. "Nothing's wrong. Not really. It's just that your father has traded off our beautiful team of horses for a no-good team of bays." Quietly, almost to herself, she added, "Fox was such a beauty. Why did I ever marry a horse trader?"

With a sinking heart, Cliff thought of the reddish-gold gelding with the white-stocking feet and a blaze on his face.

After drying her eyes on a corner of her apron, Mama looked at Cliff. "I shouldn't have said that. I really do love your father." Without further comment, she busied herself in the kitchen.

Bewildered by this sudden development, Cliff stood before the kitchen window reflecting on this new situation and gazing across the green pastures and fields to the snow-capped mountains in the distance. He knew that the team of trotting horses had been his mother's pride and joy.

Floyd's voice suddenly interrupted his thoughts.

"Hey, Cliff! Come out and see the new team Papa just bought." Reluctantly Cliff joined his brother, and the two boys headed for the barn. "One of 'em's an outlaw!" Floyd added, nearly bursting with excitement.

"Really?" Cliff asked, showing new interest in the situation.

"Sure enough. She killed a man. That's how Papa got 'er so cheap."

Their father met them at the barn door.

"Don't you boys go near those horses," his stern voice warned.

And there, in the same stall where Red and Fox had so recently stood, was a team of bays. One mare was very gentle, father told them. But the one called Topsy carried a reputation like the gunmen of Grandpa's day: she had killed a man.

"So that's Topsy," Cliff mused, folding his arms over his chest. "She dosen't look mean to me. I'll bet her owner had been mean to 'er," he reasoned.

"Just the same, you keep away from her," his father ordered. "She just might kick, or she could strike quick as lightning with her front feet." He picked up a pitchfork and tossed the horses some hay.

Cliff dared not say anything about it, but he had a hankering to help Topsy adjust to her new home. He decided to start with a few acts of kindness.

In the days that followed, when no one else was around, he would scoop up a handful of oats and toss it into her feedbox. Topsy responded at once. Whenever she saw Cliff coming into the barn or approaching the corral, she would give a soft whinny. Love gradually begat love, and in a very short time she came right up to the gate to see if he might have a carrot or a piece of bread to share with her. Then he stroked her soft neck gently.

Later in the spring, Father won the bid on a job to gravel the streets of the little Montana town of Three Forks near the headwaters of the Missouri River. With three teams and wagons and two hired men, he prepared to set off, leaving Cliff and Floyd to take care of things at home. Of course they were eager to go along and assured their father that they were big enough to shovel gravel.

"Well, let's see," he responded. "If you both went with me, who would help at home?" That made them feel they were needed, and it was a nice way of saying No. There wouldn't be any shoveling of gravel by hand, anyway, he assured them. It would all be hauled with dump wagons, and a road grader would spread it on the streets.

But Cliff's disappointment soon turned to pleasure at the thought of looking after Topsy. She would be lonely when all the other horses were away. His mother also shared his devotion to the horse, and he noticed the little attentions she gave Topsy.

Mother had established an early reputation as an expert horsewoman. Prior to her marriage she always drove her own horses. The single harness which she had used on Belle, her driving horse, was carefully stored along with her own buggy in the barn.

One day while Father was away at Three Forks, Mother found she needed some things from town. Of course, whenever she needed to run errands or wanted to shop, Grandpa Rouse, who lived nearby, would take her. But this time she had other plans. Perhaps her cowgirl upbringing led her to believe she could handle Topsy for herself for this trip. She told Cliff she had decided to hitch Topsy to her buggy. She was satisfied, she said, that Topsy had proven to be a gentle and manageable horse. Besides, she added, her trip with the horse would be a surprise to Father when he came home. Why bother her in-laws to run errands for her?

Fearing that Topsy would become excited, Mother would not allow either Cliff or Floyd to help her harness Topsy or hitch the horse to the buggy. So Cliff watched silently, his eagerness dampened by his mother's caution.

"You boys stand back while I hitch Topsy. She has never been driven single before, and I don't know what she might do."

"Mama doesn't act excited or talk scared," Floyd whispered.

"I know," Cliff agreed, "and Topsy listens to her. She knows all that Mama says." He wasn't too sure of Topsy's intentions, but he admired his mother's ability to handle the horse.

He watched as the shafts were raised and fastened and the tugs hooked. Topsy stood motionless, just like an experienced horse, and when Mother picked up the lines and stepped into the buggy, the mare moved off with ease, as if she had done that sort of thing all her life. Cliff followed the buggy to the hitching post at the front of the house and waited while his mother went inside to change her clothes for town.

"Mama, may I go with you?" Cliff asked politely, as she took the reins and settled herself into the buggy seat.

"No, Son. I want you to stay here and help take care of the house while I am gone. If you will help Floyd take care of the younger children, I will bring you something from town."

Cliff knew better than to beg, and as Topsy left the yard at a brisk trot, he turned away quickly so Mother would not see his tears of disappointment.

It seemed like a long time before Topsy wheeled into the yard again. Mother stepped down from the buggy with several paper-wrapped packages in her hands and then unloaded a huge box of groceries. She hadn't forgotten the treat she had promised. Soon the children's mouths and faces reflected their enjoyment of the licorice she had brought them.

Then she told them about her trip to town. Everything had gone well with Topsy until they descended a hill, crossed a little creek, and started up the other side of the grade.

When Topsy began the pull up the steepest part of the hill, the buggy shafts dropped down. Mother at once drew up the lines and called, "Whoa!" Topsy stopped at once and waited calmly while Mother blocked the buggy wheels with rocks so it could not roll backward.

Then she commanded Topsy to back up a step or two so the shafts could be put into place again and the tugs tightened a notch. She sighed with relief at the mare's obedience, realizing that if the horse had become excited there could have been a serious runaway.

"Bless old Topsy," she said, as Cliff listened solemnly. "That's what I call horse sense."

Cliff gave a sigh of relief also, proud that his mother had handled the situation so calmly and determined to be as good with horses as she.

When Father returned home from the graveling job at Three Forks, he was indeed surprised when he found that Mother had been driving Topsy hitched to the buggy. As soon as he could spare a little time, he saddled and rode Topsy. She seemed gentle and well behaved. Before long he allowed Cliff to ride her, and she was a joy to ride. Cliff wondered how it happened that she had come to the ranch with a bad reputation that seemed to follow her everywhere, in spite of her good present behavior.

One day not long afterward, Father needed a team of workhorses from the pasture. "Floyd—Clifford—I want you to go out to the pasture and get Deck and Don. Take their halters and some oats, and they will come right to you."

"May we take Topsy?" Cliff asked, hesitating. "It's at least a mile to the pasture."

"If you hitch her to the buggy, you may, but I don't want you riding that mare and leading horses behind her. If a rope should get under her tail, you could have a Wild West show right quick; and somebody might get hurt."

Always glad for the opportunity to drive Topsy, the boys quickly harnessed the horse. With the halter ropes and a few oats in a bucket, they started for the pasture with Topsy and the buggy. After tying her to a fencepost near the gate, they went up the hill looking for Deck and Don. Soon they found the horses and led them toward the pasture gate. There the boys' grandfather met them.

"Where's your father?" Grandpa inquired.

"He's at home," the boys replied.

"Who drove that horse?" Grandpa asked, motioning to Topsy.

"I did," Floyd answered.

"Well!" their grandfather answered in surprise. "Your Pa should know better than that.

She's not safe for boys to handle." He paused. "Get in," he motioned toward the buggy. "I'll drive her home."

Cliff hopped on the back of the buggy, holding the team's halter ropes in his hands. Floyd untied Topsy and quickly stepped into the buggy. Before he could sit down, Topsy took off like a racehorse at the shot of a gun, with a burst of speed that amazed even Grandpa. He braced his feet against the dashboard, his face grim as he took a viselike grip on the reins, and away they dashed for home.

Cliff, sitting with his feet hanging over the endgate of the buggy and his hands holding the halter ropes for Deck and Don, was yanked off the buggy with Topsy's first leap. The slow-paced workhorses were not ready for a race and needed more time to get under way.

A few minutes later Mother looked out the kitchen window and gave a little gasp. Topsy raced into the dooryard with the buggy careening on two wheels. The plucky little bay drew up to the hitching post, a cloud of dust following her, as she skidded to an abrupt halt.

"Where's Clifford?" Mother called anxiously.

"I don't know," Floyd exclaimed, turning around on the buggy seat. "He was on the back of the buggy when we started home." He jumped to the ground, walking back to the yard gate, and looked down the road toward the pasture. There came Cliff, plodding along, leading the two workhorses.

"I tell you, Pearl, that horse is plumb dangerous!" Grandpa almost shouted. "I don't know why in the world Lee ever let those boys drive her. He ought to know better than that." He shook his head and started walking toward home, mumbling to himself.

His whole family seemed to revolve around horses, and for Cliff to dream of the horses in his future came quite naturally. Cliff often heard his grandfather tell how he had spent much of his first thirty years in the West on horseback. Cliff's father later went into partnership with Grandpa, and together they bought and sold horses. Cliff could not remember his first horseback ride—he had been too young.

Before automobiles and tractors, all farm work and transportation was horsepowered. Automobiles were just coming into general use when Cliff was a boy. Occasionally a car would drive past his grandparents' house. If he happened to be visiting there, Cliff would run out to the road and smell the tracks, like a dog sniffing a rabbit's trail. He was intrigued by the smell of the exhaust, thinking it came from the wheel tracks.

About that time Cliff's Uncle Claude

bought a Maxwell touring car with jump seats. Cliff marveled at it. The driver sat on the right side, and the gearshift lever was outside on the running board. It had a shiny brass radiator and carbide lights.

Even so, nearly everyone still had driving horses and work teams. Most of the horses that traveled the hard roads were shod to keep their hooves in good condition. Many of them were brought to the blacksmith shop owned by Cliff's Uncle Claude to be shod. Cliff loitered around the blacksmith shop whenever he could, helping with things that a boy could do.

Working at the blacksmith's shop one day, resetting the iron tires on the wheels of his wagon, Father looked up from his work to see Cliff lugging an old saddle toward the shop. Just then Uncle Claude stepped to the door, and the two men watched the boy struggling along with his oversize load.

"Where do you suppose the saddle is going with that boy?" Uncle Claude asked with a grin.

Then father recognized the saddle. "What are you doing with Grandpa's old saddle, Son?"

"Grandpa told me I could use it, so I want to get it fixed up, "Cliff answered.

"It needs a lot of fixing, all right," his father observed. "No cinch, no stirrups."

"Grandpa said it had a lot of 'sentimility,' but I couldn't see anything about it that looked so bad," Cliff replied.

The two men smiled at Cliff's misunderstood word. Cliff remembered that Grandpa had said he had used the saddle when he worked as an Indian scout for the U.S. Army along with Jim Bridger—an old frontiersman and trailblazer of the West.

"That old leather needs some limbering up," Uncle Claude commented, rubbing the stiff straps with his strong hands.

Cliff looked up at his uncle. "Do you have some leather limberer?"

"You just take some mutton or beef tallow," Uncle Claude instructed, "and rub it into the leather. Work it in with your hands till it feels soft again. It will take a lot of rubbing," he warned.

"I think there are some old stirrups and cinches in the harness room," Father added. "Go find Grandpa and see if he will help you find the right parts."

It wasn't long before Cliff returned to the blacksmith shop with his hands full of saddle parts that Grandpa had given him. Grandpa donated the tallow. Floyd came along too, carrying some of the old cinches and straps. Since they were fixing up Grandpa's saddle so they could use it, Floyd said it might as well have two cinches on it, like all the Montana and Wyoming cowboys used on their saddles.

Several days later, while his father was plowing and Floyd was away helping Grandpa plant potatoes, Cliff took down Grandpa's saddle and put it on Topsy, not noticing how she humped her back during the process. After tightening the cinch straps, Cliff put his foot in the stirrup, grabbed the saddle horn, and swung up into the seat.

Then, unexpectedly, Topsy began to buck. It happened so fast that Cliff, taken by surprise, went sailing over her head and landed on the ground in a heap. He lay there, shocked and humiliated, with the breath knocked out of him. Soon he saw Mother coming on the run, calling, "Are you hurt?" Then he began to cry.

After being so shaken up, Cliff felt sure he had a serious injury of some kind. But when his father examined him, he could find no damage.

"Aw, you're not hurt," he told Cliff sternly. "Topsy just crow-hopped a little. Now get up and quit your bawling. The best medicine for you is to get right back on that horse and ride 'er."

Cliff dusted off his overalls and cautiously mounted again. Topsy seemed jittery but she calmed down as he sat on her back.

"I wonder what was the matter with her, Papa?" Cliff asked.

17

" 'Twas probably that double cinch you boys put on that saddle," his father observed. "Topsy isn't used to it. When the Montana cowboys used to go to Pendleton in the early days, they would buy Oregon horses to use on their cattle drives. When they put their double-cinch saddles on those horses, they expected to have a Wild West show."

"Even broke horses?" Cliff wondered.

"Sure—at least they were sold for broke horses," his father said with a chuckle.

"Did the Oregon cowboys use single-cinch saddles?"

"That's what I've been told."

Cliff hesitated for a few moments.

"Do you think I should take that back cinch off?" he asked.

"That won't be necessary now that Topsy has become accustomed to it. She won't buck with you again," Father told him. But next time you saddle a horse, you better watch out for warning signals."

"What do you mean by warning signals?"

"Oh, like when she lays her ears back or humps her back or dances around."

"Well—she did act kind of strange," Cliff admitted, looking away sheepishly. "I should have known. Wow! She sure did surprise me."

A Cowboy Goes to School

Fritz, the family dog, had been lassoed so many times that whenever he saw Cliff with a rope in his hands, he would slink away and hide. Cliff's young sisters had complained to Mother repeatedly about being Cliff's victims, and she finally forbade his roping the other children.

It was clear that Cliff loved horses and anything that had to do with them. Even at the age of three or four, his vivid imagination pictured him as the proud owner of a team of sleek, black horses. He often told his older brother of the beautiful horses he owned.

"Where do you keep your team?" Floyd asked one day. "I haven't seen them."

Cliff would point out a distant mountain ridge. "Just over the other side of that mountain."

"And when do you ride them?"

"At night, when everybody is asleep."

When he was older, Cliff still dreamed of

horses and cowboys, and since Topsy had come to the ranch, all he wanted to do was ride.

One hot day when the garden needed weeding and the potatoes needed hoeing, Mother made Cliff and Floyd a proposition.

"If you boys will work in the garden until noon, I'll fix you a picnic lunch, and you can have the rest of the day off to do whatever you want."

So the boys tackled the work willingly and accomplished more by noon than they would ordinarily have done in a full day.

"Let's take Topsy and go fishing up Bear Creek," Floyd suggested. That sounded good to Cliff—as long as he could ride the horse.

"Be sure you have a jackknife," Cliff reminded his brother.

The boys had no factory-made fishing poles. Each would find a straight, limber willow whip and attach his fishline and hook to the end of it.

They didn't take precious time to saddle Topsy, but with just her bridle and lines they set off to Bear Creek. A little way above the old Bear Creek schoolhouse they rode across the creek, cut two willow poles, and fastened on their lines and hooks.

"What are we going to use for bait?" Cliff wondered. They had no worms or grasshoppers.

"Hellgrammites," Floyd announced.

Both boys scrambled along the shore of the creek, overturning the stones, looking for the dark-brown larva that lived under the moist rocks at the water's edge. They soon found plenty.

Bear Creek, however, was not noted for its abundance of sizable fish. When Floyd caught his first fish, he excitedly jerked it high into the air.

Cliff laughed so much he had to hold his stomach. "At first there, Floyd, I thought it was a bird!" he croaked.

Farther and farther up the creek they wandered, and the afternoon passed all too quickly. It seemed they had just begun fishing when the time came to go home and do their evening chores.

For the afternoon's effort they caught only two fish, but they were happy with what they had accomplished. Astride Topsy, the boys looked for the best place to cross the creek and start home.

The banks of Bear Creek were high and steep this far up the canyon, and only a short cattle trail led down to the water. The boys followed it and guided Topsy across the stream. But on the opposite side was a very steep bank, with no trail leading up from the creek. Topsy made a few lunges and reached the top of the grade, but at the same time both riders slipped backwards off her rump and were dumped into the creek.

Dripping wet, unhappy, and fearing that Topsy might start home without them, they scrambled up the bank too, their bare toes digging into the soft soil. There at the top stood Topsy, looking at them in an apologetic way as if to say," Sorry, fellows, but I couldn't help it."

They remounted and Topsy headed for home.

Life in rural Montana had its share of routine as well as its share of surprises and minor disasters for the Rouse family.

Early one Friday morning Mother called to Cliff, "I need you to help churn the butter this morning."

After she helped him start the churning, she went out to gather vegetables from the garden. Cliff chugged the dasher of the churn up and down, up and down; and he had pleasant visions of the cool buttermilk he soon would drink.

Suddenly his peaceful thoughts were interupted by a loud commotion in the garden.

"Get out of here!" he heard his mother shout. "Go get 'em, Fritz! Clifford! Clifford, help get these cows out of the garden."

Cliff rushed out the back door and ran toward the garden, where he saw the neighbor's cows dashing here and there, grabbing bites of vegetables as they ran. Fritz seemed to sense the urgency of the situation and, barking fiercely and nipping at their heels, quickly drove the cows away. But what a mess they left behind! The corn patch suffered the most damage. What stalks hadn't been eaten were knocked down, and nearly the whole garden was trampled over.

"Now, if that isn't a mess!" Mother fretted in exasperation as she surveyed the disaster. Perhaps she would have cried had she not been so angry.

"Clifford, will you drive those cows home? If you don't, they will be right back in the garden again. Go on," she said, "I'll take care of the churning myself."

Cliff and Fritz drove the cattle back up the dusty lane to the Watson place. Cliff spotted the hole in the fence where the cattle had slipped out; so he drove them into the corral and closed the gate. He didn't see anyone around the house or barn.

A few minutes after returing home, he saw Elder George Watson walking briskly towards the house. Watson was the president of the Montana Conference of the Seventh-day Adventists. Cliff was afraid he was coming in anger over the rather brusque treatment his cows just received. But Watson came to apologize for the trouble his cows had caused and to pay for the damages. After talking with

Mother, he turned to Cliff.

"You were a good boy to drive my cows home and close the gate." He slipped a quarter into Cliff's hand.

Little rain fell that summer, and the merciless sun scorched and withered the pasture grass. Within a few days Watson's cows were out again. They came to the Rouse garden, but this time they couldn't get in. Cliff and Floyd had stretched wire through the brush and barricaded the place where the cows had scrambled through before. Cliff noticed them peering longingly through the bushes toward the garden and sent Fritz to chase them back up the lane.

Watson soon noticed that his cows were missing again and went looking for them.

"Did my cows get in your garden again?" he inquired anxiously.

"No," Cliff replied. "I drove them back up the lane before they had a chance."

Watson nodded, looking thoughtfully at Cliff. "How would you and your brother like to herd my cows for me?" he asked. My pasture is all eaten down, and I can't keep them in."

"That would be great!" Cliff answered eagerly, "but I don't know if my folks will let me."

"I'll talk to your father," Watson said, "and see if he can spare you boys. If he can, I'll make it worth your time."

Within the next day or two Cliff and Floyd got the job of herding the Watson's cows and also a few for T. G. Johnson, another neighbor.

The boys herded the cattle along the lanes and rights-of-way during the rest of the summer. Soon their neighbors' boys, Paul and Byrle Rittenhouse, went along, herding their own milch cows. The boys had a good time together.

"Elder Watson has really made a hit with Clifford," Mother commented to Mrs. Rittenhouse one day.

"Isn't that good!" she agreed. "He seems like a fine Christian man. Our children like to hear him preach."

"Clifford even wants to be a minister like Elder Watson," she continued. "Now, that is really something! I figured all he ever thought about was horses and cowboys. This is the first indication we've had that he is interested in spiritual things."

"Well, who knows?" Mother's friend exclaimed. "Clifford may be a preacher someday."

"I just hope he keeps that desire through his teenage years," Mother sighed, shaking her head. "That seems to be their hardest time, when so many temptations come to young people."

"It's like my husband and I were saying just

the other day," Mrs. Rittenhouse concluded. "If we can get them safely over fool's hill, then maybe they will settle down and use some sense."

Mount Ellis Academy, not far from the Rouse home, had the loyalty of Montana Seventh-day Adventist families, to whom education in a Christain school was a prime concern. The academy held a special meaning for the Rouses. Cliff often heard stories of its pioneering days and how it had been established to bring high-quality Christian education to the Adventist youngsters of Montana. The influence of the school helped to broaden their outlook on the world mission of their church.

Although Lee Rouse never attended the school, he strongly supported the educational system as practiced at the academy. He bought a piece of property, built a house, and moved his family there, intending to educate his children through all the grades at Mount Ellis.

Lack of finances created many problems in the early years and called for sacrifice on the part of teachers, parents, and students. Before Cliff started first grade, it seemed certain the school would be forced to close.

Then two former students, who attended Walla Walla College in Washington, offered to return to Mount Ellis to lend their support.

They developed ideas they felt would place the school on a better financial basis.

The school board voted favorably on their propositions, and soon Victor Armstrong, assisted by Stephen Palmer, headed the staff at the academy. The school board followed Armstrong's suggestion and purchased more land. Students who needed financial aid were able to attend classes and work as well, in order to pay their school expenses. To create opportunity for more student employment, one portion of the school property was devoted to the operation of a country store.

One of the most progressive aspects of the Armstrong—Palmer administration might be correctly termed the "good—neighbor policy." Cliff remembered some of the details of the plan as it was discussed at home. He remembered how Armstrong fostered a community literary society. All the neighbors—Adventist and non-Adventist alike—were invited to have a part in the organization. Meetings were held one Saturday night a month in the main auditorium at the academy. There seemed to be no shortage of talent or participation, and the society did much to unify the community and to create good will.

One interesting sidelight of Armstrong's policy showed up early one spring. The winter had been harsher than usual, and everyone welcomed the warmth of spring. The sight of wild flowers on the hillsides seemed to bring new life to the community and a friendly interest in outdoor recreation.

Nearly every Sunday, if the ground was dry enough, the men of the community organized into opposing teams and played baseball, while the onlookers helped prepare refreshments and also comprised the cheering section. Sometimes the teams competed at the Bear Creek Canyon school grounds and sometimes at Mount Ellis.

Near the close of the school term, Mount Ellis Academy hosted an end-of-school picnic. On this special occasion the parents of the students, as well as all friends in the community, were encouraged to come out and enjoy the day.

The academy enrollment at that time was the largest it had ever been, with about 200 students; and the picnic promised to be a great event. Large kettles of food were brought from the school kitchen. A huge kettle of lemonade stood at the end of the table. A long-handled dipper hung on a nail beside the container, and everyone wishing a little refreshment just helped himself.

During the morning hours the men played horseshoes, and the boys entertained themselves on improvised baseball diamonds in the meadow. Soon the dinner gong sounded, and the games came to a speedy halt.

Cliff looked up and down the long line of tables and wondered where to begin. He saw almost every kind of food imaginable— salads, pickles, preserves, jam and jellies for bread and rolls, cold fried chicken, slices of roast beef, baked beans, cottage cheese, freezers full of various kinds of ice cream, cakes, pies, pudding. Grandma Rouse brought her popular banana-cream cake with whipped-cream frosting. What a day for hungry boys and girls! Cliff ate until he couldn't hold another bite.

After the misery of overeating subsided, the single fellows played a game of baseball against the married men. The single men lost, but they all had a lot of fun.

Then the looked-for match between the men of Bear Creek Canyon School District and the men of Mount Ellis Academy became the center of attraction as the teams took the field. But the Bear Creek team was short one player. The team members looked around for a recruit and spotted Cliff's father.

Father hadn't played on either team, but some of his neighbors who had attended high school with him in Bozeman knew he was a good player. Two members of the team approached him as he stood on the sideline.

"Lee, we need a good shortstop. Will you help us out?"

"Well—I haven't played for a long time,"

Father hesitated, "but I'll do my best if you want me."

As father accompanied the other players to the field, Cliff and Floyd were delighted. They knew how much their father loved to play baseball.

As the game progressed, the teams seemed to be very closely matched. Both sides, of course, did their best and mixed a lot of playful bantering into the game, while the spectators rooted with great enthusiasm. The scores mounted high, with quite a number of home runs. Whenever someone made a good play he drew applause, regardless of which side he represented.

Soon it was Father's turn to bat, and Cliff noted with admiration his powerful muscles as he gripped the bat and eyed the pitcher.

"'It a 'ome, won, Papa!" called out little Alberta, Cliff's youngest sister.

"Strike one!" bellowed the umpire.

Swish!

"Strike two!"

Father gripped the bat, took a home-run stance, and looked hard at the pitcher. The pitch came in right over the plate, and he swung hard.

Swish!

"Str-r-r-ike three," the umpire bawled.

Amidst the mixture of groans and cheers, Cliff and Floyd looked down, kicking aimlessly at the grass, feeling very deflated.

But by the time he had another chance at bat, father seemed to have studied the pitcher's technique; and he hit a solid home run, bringing in one base runner as well.

As the game entered the final inning, the score was tied at twenty-one runs each. As the last half of the final inning began, Bear Creek led by one run. Could they hold that lead when Mount Ellis came to bat?

The first Mount Ellis batter got a single. The second batter got a base on balls. The third batter came to the plate, two men on bases and nobody out. It seemed to Cliff that the pitcher was tiring. Everybody was tense.

The batter hit the first pitch squarely—too high for the shortstop, and the runner on second base dashed for third. Just then Father seemed to have springs in his legs as he leaped high into the air and caught the fly ball in his extended glove. He came down on second base and tagged the runner from first.

The game was over just that quickly.

A few seconds passed in an astonished hush before anyone realized exactly what had happened. Then the players from both teams rushed over to Father and thumped his back in delight, until Cliff worried that his father might get hurt. But Cliff's father felt relieved and proud as he was carried off the field on the shoulders of his teammates.

A Country Boy in Town

After the hard winter of 1918-1919, Father decided to plant a crop of wheat. He spent long hours preparing the soil and seeding the grain. With a wheat crop and a large garden, he hoped his family would have provisions to last through the coming year. Cliff and Floyd were strong and proved to be good helpers. The girls, though younger, were also willing workers.

But a problem arose with baby brother Wayne. Mother tried every way she knew to find food that agreed with him. But despite her best efforts, the little fellow seemed to be starving. Something must be found soon that would nourish him. In her daily devotions, Mother prayed that God would give her wisdom in caring for her baby.

While preparing the table for dinner one day, she placed little Wayne in a high chair by the table and soon came from the kitchen with a heaping dish of mashed potatoes. She placed the dish just a little too close, and after she went away for the other food, the baby reached out and helped himself to the potatoes. Before she could stop him, his little mouth was filled.

"Well!" exclaimed Mother. "If that doesn't make him sick, he can have all the potatoes he wants!" The mashed potatoes seemed to digest with no problem.

In those days mothers were very hesitant to begin giving their babies solid food. They were fed only liquids until they were at least a year old. But as soon as Wayne ate solid food, he began to thrive.

The summer weather grew hot and dry, and Father worried about his wheat. "If we don't get some rain pretty soon," he told a neighbor, "my wheat will be ruined."

By August he knew his wheat would produce little or no grain. He decided it would at least make some hay; so he cut and stacked it for winter feeding of the livestock.

On one of August's especially hot days, the boys took a break from their work. "Come on, Cliff," Floyd called. "Mama said we could go swimming." So the boys started off with Fritz toward the creek. They found a natural swimming pool in the meandering creek, fed by mountain streams flowing down through the foothills. Although the farmland was parched and barren, the creek continued to

33

flow, and the boys enjoyed its cool refreshment.

After Cliff swam for a short period, he became tired, climbed out of the pool, and lay on the creek bank to rest. Although the sun felt extremely hot, he didn't have the ambition or the desire to get back into the water. By the time Floyd finished his swim and dressed, Cliff felt so sick that he could hardly walk back to the house.

Mother was worried after taking his temperature and finding it to be 105 degrees. She sent for the doctor, who called his sickness "summer complaint." Cliff stayed in bed for over a week, too sick to care about or even notice what took place around him. Baby Wayne often came creeping to the open door, smiling at him in his sweet, winning way; but Cliff felt too sick to respond.

Before Cliff fully recovered, Alberta, his youngest sister, became ill with what seemed to be the same ailment. The Sabbath morning before her illness struck, all members of the family except Cliff went to Sabbath School and church. On the way home Alberta stood behind the buggy seat, watching her father drive the horses.

"I'm not going to Sabbath School anymore," she stated impulsively. Her mother asked why. Alberta just shrugged her shoulders, making no reply. Her parents wondered about this sudden declaration, because she had always enjoyed Sabbath School.

The next morning Alberta complained of feeling sick. By noon her fever reached a dangerous level, and her condition did not improve throughout the afternoon. Dr. Smith came to see her but seemed at a loss to find a medication that would help.

All during the week Alberta's fever raged, and she seemed to slip away a little more each day. On Friday morning Mother somehow felt that her little girl would not live to see another day. She called for Father, and they tried to comfort and strengthen each other and console the other children throughout those trying hours. Cliff could sense the seriousness of his sister's condition but could only stand beside her bed helplessly.

At last all the children and then Mother and Father bade Alberta goodbye, but she did not show any sign of recognition. At about five o'clock in the afternoon her breathing ceased, and her brief life ended.

Mother had maintained a strong front of courage throughout those days of suffering, but after Alberta's death she could endure no longer and broke into uncontrollable weeping. Father placed his strong arms around her tenderly and led her from the room.

A kind neighbor built a small, beautiful coffin; and Alberta was laid to rest in the

Rouse family plot in the Bozeman cemetery.

During the years prior to Alberta's death, the family members, all working together, had created a happy, secure home atmosphere; but now it seemed that Mother could not endure this bitter loss. Father gave her the money to travel to Livingston to visit her foster mother, and her two youngest children went with her.

After Mother went away, Cliff—and Floyd and Father—felt the loss more keenly too; so they closed up the big empty ranch house and moved to a little shack in nearby Bear Canyon, where they worked in a lath mill Father had built several years before. The boys worked steadily, right along with their father, every day except the Sabbath.

That fall Floyd went to stay with his grandparents so he could attend church school at Mount Ellis. Cliff stayed on with his father at the mill. Father brought Cliff's schoolbooks and assignments home. He planned for Cliff to do his schoolwork every morning, and then, if he had completed his work, he could help at the mill in the afternoon.

The plan sounded good, but Cliff found it hard to keep up his enthusiasm for it. Consequently, most of his assignments were never done. He preferred work at the mill with his father or other work at the cabin. It appeared that unless he was supervised, he could not generate much interest in his schoolwork.

He started working arithmetic problems one morning and found he needed further help. But with no help available at the moment, he returned to the job of getting dinner ready for his father and the hired men. He often saw his father make biscuits and knew the recipe from memory. And he knew how to peel and boil potatoes and make gravy.

When the men came in from the mill at noon, dinner was ready and the table was set. As the men washed, Cliff pulled the pan of hot, golden buscuits from the oven and set potatoes and gravy on the table. His father helped him get the rest of the meal together, and they sat down to eat. The men were so impressed with Cliff's success in the kitchen that from then on he had a full-time job— cook, dishwasher, and housekeeper.

That spring Father took Cliff and Floyd to the town of Livingston to visit their mother. She cried for joy as she hugged her growing boys.

One of the first things she did after their arrival in town was to take them to a barbershop for haircuts—the first time either of the boys had ever been to a professional barber.

Father and Mother were planning to return to the home place in time to plant a garden and get the farm work under control for the growing season. But from his parents' conversation, Cliff concluded that Aunt Cindy (as he called his mother's foster mother) had suffered a recent stroke and was partially paralyzed. Mother and Father offered to take her to their home at Mount Ellis, but she felt she must stay in Livingston to look after her property a while longer.

A few days later Cliff watched sadly as his father and Floyd left the rest of the family in Livingston, to make the trip back home to Mount Ellis. With Topsy hitched to the buggy, they drove away from Aunt Cindy's yard, and he watched longingly until they turned at the street corner. Then he walked into the house and slumped dejectedly into the chair. He wished he could just go to sleep and wake up with all the family together and happy once more, as they were before Alberta's death.

An ominous feeling that he could not explain came over him. If only he had a key, he wished to himself, that would unlock the future. He wondered what lay ahead.

Livingston, a small town about twenty-five miles east of Bozeman, boasted at that time a population of about 4000. It was a hub of the Northern Pacific Railroad and the center of the ranching country. The town's atmosphere seemed to hum with activity. A spur of the Northern Pacific line branched off near Livingston and ran to Gardiner.

Life in town was exciting to a boy from the country—at least for a time. Cliff had no chores to do, such as carrying water and wood. Just once a day the coal scuttle was filled. It seemed to him that Aunt Cindy had all the modern conveniences—even an indoor toilet. He was used to the kerosene lamps which must be filled with oil and the tall glass chimneys which were cleaned and polished every day. He was amazed the first night at Aunt Cindy's house when the electric lights were turned on.

"It's just about as light as daytime," he remarked, as he looked in wonder at the electric cord which hung from the ceiling. When a switch on the light socket was turned, the bulb lighted just like magic. It seemed almost unbelievable to Cliff.

One of Mother's cousins, Earl Hanson, stopped at Aunt Cindy's house one day, driving a new Ford touring car as shiny black as a newly polished kitched range.

"How do you like it, Pearl?" he asked.

Mother stood looking with admiration.

"This top can be let down in just a few minutes," he explained. "It has side curtains, too, in case a rainstorm comes up. They fasten on with these little gadgets here." He pointed to the metal snaps on the car's body.

Cliff came running to see the new Model T.

"How would you like a ride in it?" Earl

asked. Cliff looked in wonder at the imitation leather seats and the black canvas top with its three isinglass windows in the rear.

Before his mother had a chance to answer, Cliff shouted, "I would! I sure would!" He jumped up and down to emphasize his delight and enthusiasm.

"How about tomorrow evening when I get off work?"

The time was agreed upon, and how the day dragged by as Cliff waited. He felt sure the clock must be nearly run down, its tired hands moved so slowly.

He thought of the old Maxwell parked in the buggy shed at Grandpa's place, with its brass radiator, steering wheel on the right-hand side, and the gearshift outside on the running board. But this new Ford of cousin Earl's— it even had electric lights! Earl also said a new self-starter was expected on the market soon, even though his new car would start with just a quarter turn of the crank.

When Cousin Earl and his wife finally drove up to the gate in the new flivver, Cliff came bounding out of the house and right into the back seat.

"Just look at that. Cliff's rarin' to go!" Cousin Earl exclaimed. "Where are the rest of the folks?" he asked.

"They're coming," Cliff assured him; and in a minute or two Mother appeared with Aunt

Cindy supported on her arm. In all her eighty-six years this would be her first ride in an automobile.

"Is this all the people that are coming?" Cousin Earl sounded almost disappointed.

"Bernice promised to stay at home with the baby," Mother explained.

"Oh, bring them along," he urged. "There's plenty of room for all."

Cliff sprang from the back seat without even opening the door and dashed into the house. He reappeared with baby Wayne and his happy sister.

As soon as they were seated, the Ford went roaring down the street in low gear. As Cousin Earl released his foot from the pedal, it leaped forward in high gear.

They rode through town and out the river road toward Aunt Cindy's old house at Pine Creek. Cliff watched dreamily as the fence posts seemed to go whizzing by them. Near the bridge across the Yellowstone River, Cousin Earl slowed the car and turned it around. When they started toward town once again, a soft breeze played across the riders' faces as the car picked up speed.

As the evening shadows lowered, Cousin Earl turned on the headlights. Cliff noted that they weren't as bright as the lights on the old Chalmers his father and Uncle Claude used to own at Mount Ellis, but he said nothing about that. He didn't want to downgrade Cousin Earl's new Ford.

All too soon they were back in town, and the car stopped at Aunt Cindy's place again. Everyone, including little Wayne, thanked Cousin Earl for the ride.

When school started in the fall, Cliff felt like a stranger in the town school, but the children soon lost their awkwardness and got acquainted quickly. He found that the Livingston boys were just as rowdy and rough as his former schoolmates had been.

Through the manual training program in the Livingston school, Cliff learned to use woodworking tools. He made a number of useful articles for his mother, including a breadboard which she used for many years. He also made a lamp and took it home to her for a Christmas present.

He enjoyed making cutouts with the coping saw. He drew and cut out horses that he liked to think resembled Topsy. The little wooden horse gave him a deep longing for the free and easy life of the ranch where he used to be so happy.

Father's visits to Livingston became longer and more frequent, as he found it increasingly difficult to be separated from his wife and children.

"When do you think you will be able to come home?" he asked repeatedly.

"I wish I could go tomorrow, but—" Mother hesitated, "Aunt Cindy is so feeble yet. The doctor says she could have another stroke at any time."

After hearing the conversation, Cliff became more and more dissatisfied with town life and his family's uncertain situation. He knew his father was lonely and feared he might sell the ranch and move to Livingston.

His fears were not ungrounded. One day soon after, Mother received a thick envelope and a letter stating that Father had sold the ranch, and he was enclosing the legal papers for her to sign.

When his mother told him about it, Cliff felt that the end of the world had come.

Where Is Home Now?

Cliff felt that his father had made a grave mistake in selling the ranch at Mount Ellis; but it did have one good aspect—the family was delighted to be together again.

The year 1921 found the Rouse family of six, plus Aunt Cindy, cramped into a small two-bedroom house. For the two oldest boys the charm and newness of life in town soon gave way to a feeling of restricted freedom.

Grandpa and Grandma Rouse arrived early one afternoon from the ranch at Mount Ellis. Mother prepared a meal for them while the children entertained them with news of school and play.

As they ate, Cliff noted Grandpa's comment about the creamery butter. He declared it tasted different from what they made at home.

That casual remark sent Cliff into dreaming of the times when Grandma had asked him to turn the handle of the old barrel churn. He was always glad to work patiently until the golden butter formed and floated in a sea of creamy-white buttermilk, because he knew Grandma would give him a generous amount to drink. All those thoughts made him homesick for the happy days he had spent with them in the past. He stepped out the back door and sat on the steps, his fists stuck into the pockets of his overalls.

As he sat on the porch, an idea formed in his mind as he recalled the time he and Floyd had herded the neighbors' cows at Mount Ellis. Suddenly he jumped up, eager to share his brainstorm with his older brother.

Thus it happened that Floyd and Cliff started a cattle-herding venture on the prairie and foothills near the town of Livingston. At two dollars a head per month, it soon became a profitable business operation that continued several summers, for the two ambitious farm boys.

Soon other young fellows of Livingston picked up the idea and found cattle to herd. All the cows mingled together during the day as they grazed, and in the evening each boy was responsible for getting his customers' cows back to their respective corrals. One of the boys about Cliff's age had the use of a good saddle horse; and, riding together, they could manage the cattle easily.

A number of young stock were in the herd, including some heifer calves and a big yearling steer. This husky Hereford presented himself as a challenge to the would-be cowboys.

Judging him to be gentle, Floyd one day ventured to jump on his back, just to see what the steer would do. He soon found out. After the steer gave two or three stiff-legged jumps, Floyd found himself sprawled on the ground.

The next day one of the boys came with a lariat; so they decided to stage their own rodeo. They roped the steer, and one by one the boys had their chance to ride him. Not one of them could stay on his back for more than two or three jumps.

"I can ride 'im to a standstill if you'll put a saddle on 'im," boasted one of the biggest boys loudly.

"Oh yeah? You want to bet on it?" came the challenge.

"You saddle 'im, and I'll ride 'im, just like I said I would," the braggart retorted loudly.

The boys battled to get the saddle on the husky chunk of Hereford dynamite. But finally he was tussled into the saddle; and the boaster, sitting smugly on his back, signaled for the boys to turn the yearling loose.

The big steer's hide was so loose that the saddle could turn a quarter of the way around his belly, and in less than two jumps the rider came tumbling down into the dirt.

But the frightened animal continued trying

to get rid of the thing which kept such a tight hold on his middle. At every jump he became more frantic. The boys chased him, trying to get the saddle off, until it was time to take the cattle home. They trapped him in a fence corner once and thought they could succeed in catching him, but the big red steer burst through the fence as quick as a cat with a clothespin on its tail.

When the cattle were finally rounded up and headed toward home, Cliff worried about what the owner would think when he saw his prime beef animal with a saddle on its back. He was sure he was going to lose his best customer. He simply *must* get that saddle off before he drove the steer into his owner's corral.

Cliff crept gradually closer and closer to the husky steer until at last he reached the lariat still fastened around his neck. At that moment they were approaching the old burned-out ruins of a clothing factory. Although the buildings were nearly gone, a row of hitching posts still remained.

"Hey!" If you fellows will crowd the herd over close to those posts," Cliff suggested, "I think I can get a couple of wraps around one of 'em."

So the boys urged the herd in that direction, and Cliff got a couple of dallies around a post before the steer came to the end of his rope. As soon as the boys were able to hold the year-ling, they succeeded in getting the saddle off. The lariat was quickly slipped off the steer's neck, and the animal went on his way home.

The town of Livingston—though small—proved to be less than an ideal place for grow-ing boys. The Rouse family, along with a few other Seventh-day Adventists, attended Sab-bath School in the home of one of the church members; but with few children in atten-dance, the service didn't interest the boys very much. Cliff felt it came far short of the Sabbath School and church services he had attended previously at Mount Ellis.

As the years in town passed, secular ac-tivities began to have an increasing attraction for him—the theater, the circus, the rodeo, school sports, and the carnival.

The main attraction for boys and men at the carnival was the boxing and wrestling arena. For the last event on the day's program, any boys who wished could climb into the ring and test their "dukes." When the gong sounded, the melee would begin, and the last boy on his feet would win five dollars. Urged on by his friends, Cliff tried out, along with some of the other brash boys. Like a young rooster sprouting his first tail feathers, he was learning to fight.

Cliff took a fancy to boxing when he first arrived in Livingston, and he caught on quickly. The rougher his opponents, the better he liked it. Alert and wiry, he had better success than most boys his size. Soon the gym instructor at school took an interest in him and gave him many pointers.

About that time the Dempsey-Gibbins world heavyweight championship fight—to take place in Shelby, north of Great Falls—stirred up much interest in the sport of boxing. Cliff was inspired to succeed and did well in amateur boxing, placing first in the welterweight class.

The following summer, Cliff was left in Livingston to stay with his Uncle Harvey and Aunt Ruby while his mother worked as a cook at the Mammoth Hotel in Yellowstone National Park and his father went prospecting. Cliff buddied around with a rowdy crowd and joined a gang that enjoyed fighting. He soon became involved in gang fights, one of which nearly ended in disaster.

Two rival gangs met one afternoon at an old gravel pit near the west city limits. They fought with fists, rocks, and clubs. Several of the boys were roughed up badly, but the climax came when one fellow, perched up in the rock-crushing machinery, thew a big rock, which fell on another boy's head. Blood rushed from his wound and from his mouth, and all hostilities immediately ceased as both gangs began working to revive the injured

49

boy—but to no avail. They hailed a passing car, and the injured boy was rushed to the hospital.

For several days the now-sober young "gangsters" waited anxiously. At last the boy regained consciousness. Cliff realized that their "play" might have ended with a serious blot on the characters of the boys involved in the fight.

Cliff soon left Livingston to work for the rest of the summer north of Bozeman on a wheat farm owned by another uncle. There was plenty of work on the farm for a strong young man, and his uncle welcomed the additional help. Most of the farm work was done with horses, although a few tractors were coming into use. His uncle kept about twelve work-horses, plus a driving team.

Happy to be on a farm again, Cliff enjoyed every minute of his stay. He helped put up hay, drove a team in the field while summer fallowing, and repaired fences. But most of all he enjoyed the Sunday drives with his aunt and uncle. The sleek mares—Bird and Kitten—were a well-matched team; and when hitched to the surrey, they gave the family some memorable times rolling through the countryside or up into the mountains.

Cliff worked on the farm until the wheat was cut and shocked for harvest, but he had to return to school before the threshing machine came. His mother returned home from her cook's work in Yellowstone Park, and his father came back from a fruitless summer of prospecting for a coal mine. His parents could see that their young son had grown and filled out, and they noted his browned back and solid muscles.

But Cliff had not been home long when he sensed that the home atmosphere was not warm and happy as it had been. Something was wrong, and he felt a lack of the love he had always known. It seemed that his father and mother were often irritable and bickering. What had happened? His sense of security seemed threatened, and he longed for the home he had once known.

August turned to September, and the clear, sunny autumn weather encouraged the Rouse family to look forward with new hope to the future. Many things, of course, were changed. Grandpa and Grandma Rouse didn't live at Mount Ellis anymore. Their ranch had been sold to another man, but he had agreed to rent the old homestead house at the rear of the property to Cliff's family so the boys could attend Mount Ellis Academy.

Time has a way of changing so many things, Cliff noted sadly. Aunt Cindy—at a ripe old age—was laid to rest, and her property was sold. Then there was really nothing to keep the Rouses in Livingston anymore, and Cliff's parents felt a deep concern for their family of lively "young'uns" (as his mother expressed it in her Southern way). Cliff was now constantly into trouble, and partly because of the influence of his town friends.

"A new broom sweeps clean," Mother was fond of saying, and she hoped new surroundings would help change Cliff for the better. With the old Reo truck loaded to the top of the racks with household goods, they started off for Mount Ellis again and—hopefully—for a brighter future.

That year Father leased an old coal mine up Trail Creek, three miles above the town of Chestnut. He planned to mine what coal he could and haul it to town for sale. In this way, he believed he could support his family and also supply coal for the heating plant at the academy to help pay for the boys' tuition there. On Sundays, when the boys were free, they worked together hauling coal to the school.

A friend of the family offered to give them a milch cow, and one day the boys and their father went over to the man's place on the other side of Livingston and brought her home. She was a Jersey and supplied more than enough milk and cream for the Rouse family.

Not long after that, an opportunity came to acquire three more milch cows. If the Rouses would winter them, the owner bargained, they could keep whatever profit they could make; and if they wanted to buy the cows later, a generous deal could be worked out.

"I don't have time to milk cows and clean the barn," Father told Floyd and Cliff frankly, "but if you boys will agree to milk and feed the cattle, separate the milk, and clean the barn, I'll get the cows."

"Sure we will!" the brothers agreed. "We'll take care of the cows if Mama will wash the cream separator for us."

So the matter was settled, and three more cows plus a calf were added to their growing dairy herd.

Whenever Cliff could get away from his studies and the endless chores around the barn, he enjoyed working with his father at the mine. The work was hard, but he felt rewarded that he was helping with the family's school expenses. Of course, when the ice-skating season came, he was faced with conflicting interests; but his father was understanding. He reduced Cliff's chores so that when he finished his work there was still plenty of time to head for the skating pond to spend the rest of the day.

Highlighting the school year were the occasional visits of B. M. Grandy, the conference president. His kindly smile and genuine interest in the students inspired many of them toward a life of dedicated service. He and his wife often visited Cliff's home to encourage the family in the Christian way. Their personal interest in Cliff's happiness and welfare made a lasting impression on him.

Montana winters—notoriously long and severe—often held surprises for Cliff and his brother Floyd. One icy winter day Floyd took the family truck and delivered a load of coal to an address in town. As he passed the academy on his way home, he noticed a number of students watching him as he drove through the gate of the ranch house. The driveway went past the big house, then around to the small log house where his family lived.

The driveway was grooved with deep ruts because of travel during the rainy season. The tracks were nearly filled with water, and of course, when cold weather set in, they froze solid.

Instead of slowing down as he should have, Floyd speeded up a little. He intended to apply the brakes at the last possible second and stop at the house with an impressive flourish. But to his horror, the wheels slid on the ice, and the truck smashed into the side of the house with a resounding crash.

Upon hearing the noise, several students and teachers ran up the lane to the accident scene. Unhurt but nearly sick with embarrassment, Floyd jumped out of the truck and vanished!

Even after the carpenter repaired the damage to the house and his father fixed the front of the truck as well as he could, Floyd still had a reputation for reckless driving with which to live.

But by spring the old Reo truck gave up the struggle to operate. Father replaced it with another truck—a secondhand Maxwell with rubber tires. Cliff and Floyd nicknamed it the Wreck of the Hesperus.

While attending school at Mount Ellis, Cliff's interest in music expanded and thrived. As a small boy, he had watched his mother lead the music at Sabbath School and church. He often wished that he might learn to direct music. His mother taught him the simple dynamics of conducting and sometimes played the organ while he practiced directing simple gospel songs.

N. W. Dunn soon came to Mount Ellis as the principal, and he proved to be a man of many talents. He probably was to be remembered best for his singing and musical ability. He organized musical groups which performed for many of the Sabbath services. Cliff held him in high esteem because of his God-given talent and the use he made of it.

Miss Boothby, the academy music teacher, learned of Cliff's musical interest and encouraged him to enlarge his abilities. When she felt his progress to be sufficient, she arranged for him to sing for Sabbath School and also church services. He sang the tenor part in a mixed quartet and later became the chorister for the Missionary Volunteer Society.

A lengthy letter arrived one day that autumn from Cliff's aunt who lived in Oregon. In glowing terms she related how her whole family worked in the fruit harvest.

"And just think," she concluded the letter, "that orchard is for sale. The owner wants to retire, and he will sell the orchard for just $10,000. He wants only a small down payment and will finance the rest himself. And he'll teach the buyer the fruit business."

This piece of information sparked Mother's interest. "Lee, just imagine! Instead of working so hard in that old coal mine, we could all work with the fruit." She simply bubbled with anticipation.

After more correspondence with his sister and with the owner of the orchard, Father was convinced that they should try this new venture. They sold whatever they could not take, the Maxwell was loaded with the family's possessions, and they set off for Oregon.

They traveled first into western Montana to visit relatives living in the Bitterroot Valley. Their ultimate destination was Forest Grove, Oregon, where their next home would be.

But as they were coming into the Montana town of Hamilton, the truck stalled and would not start again. Father telephoned his brother Charley, who lived south of Hamilton. He came and towed the Maxwell into town so it could be repaired.

Uncle Charley knew a mechanic who could fix the truck, and Cliff stayed with his father, who helped with the repairs. In a few days the Maxwell came out of the shop with a completely overhauled engine. The truck was back in good working condition, but its repair took a sizable chunk out of the savings for their Oregon venture.

It was haying time in the Bitterroot Valley, and Cliff went along with his father to work for a few days in the harvest to replenish their cash so they could travel on. But his father soon became interested in the local lumber industry and decided to stay in the Bitterroot area.

Disappointment and dashed hopes caused strained relationships within the family. The old bickering between his parents returned, but now it seemed to take on a more serious note.

Cliff's greatest disappointment, however, was that his parents could not afford to send him to the academy and yet would not allow him to attend the local high school. It seemed that the strong and faithful character formed at Mount Ellis was being swept away. Lacking the association of wholesome young people, he once again fell into unchristian practices and entertainment.

Discouragment clouded his mind, and he refused to attend church. He knew that he was not living a Christian life-style, and yet he did not completely lose sight of his mother's hope for him—to use his influence and talent toward the finshing of God's work. Somehow, even within the darkness of despondency, Cliff could sense that God would not forget His child.

Boiler Room Bruises

After being out of school for a year, Cliff longed to get back to Mount Ellis Academy. The more he thought about it, the more determined he became to be there by the time the autumn term began. He decided to find as much work as possible and save his money carefully.

In a short time he found work at a sawmill. Cliff and another man would fell trees until they had enough to log into the mill and saw into lumber. In the mill Cliff fired the steam boiler, which supplied power for the operation of the mill. When the work at the mill ended, he worked with a haymaking crew. Later in the summer he and Floyd picked apples.

Cliff's application to the academy was accepted, and his third-class fireman's license, secured during his work at the mill, stood him in good stead to work in the school's heating plant. He knew that his work in the fruit harvest extended well past the beginning of the term and that he would have to catch up on his homework. But he was a happy young man as he boarded the train for Bozeman and Mount Ellis Academy.

He arrived late in October, just a week before the first-period exams. He faced a mountain of homework; but as time permitted, while he tended the school boiler, he spread out his books and papers on an old desk that stood in a corner of the room.

Cliff was already acquainted with the other two student firemen. Milton took the early-morning shift, then Oran—who was not attending classes but working to build up a financial credit—took the day shift. Cliff took the last shift, working from four in the afternoon until ten in the evening, a work schedule he kept up for two years.

The Sabbath worship services seemed to be geared to Cliff's spiritual needs, and before long he too participated in the programs. Sometimes he would direct the singing or join with another student in providing special music for Sabbath School or for other meetings. Some of the students had musical instruments and volunteered to play for Sabbath School, and Cliff was appointed to be their director.

Under the guidance of the Bible teacher, J. W. Lansing, a young men's seminar was formed. Any boys interested in learning about ministerial services were invited to participate. Cliff joined the group and sometimes assisted in the church service.

Classroom appointments and homework posed major problems for Cliff, as he had to work many hours in order to meet expenses. He took only half the subjects required for sophomore status and was not officially a member of the class. But the steady grind of classes and study was broken by the pleasures of Sabbath services and Saturday-night games and programs. Like the other students, Cliff looked forward to those relaxing times.

A few of the students were able to go home for the Christmas holidays, but most of them did not have travel money and stayed on at the academy. They had fun, nevertheless, with sleigh rides, ice skating, and tobogganing.

One holiday evening the dormitory boys went into town to skate at the city rink. They walked the five miles to Bozeman, skated until the rink closed, then walked the five miles back.

While the boys were in town, the girls decided to have some fun too. They raided the boys' rooms, mixing up the bedding and removing mattresses. At 9:30 p.m. as usual the lights were turned off. Long after that hour the boys returned to their rooms, tired out and ready for a good night's sleep. But where were the beds? After considerable fumbling around in the darkness they managed to find enough mattresses and bedding to bunk down. They knew the the girls had played this prank on them—but which girls?

Before breakfast the boys agreed that they would go to the dining room but say nothing about their rooms being "rearranged," hoping some of the girls would give away the secret of who was involved in the mischief. But no hints or sly remarks were made, no evidence or clues given.

Later in the morning Milton and Cliff were at the boiler room discussing what should be done to even up the score, when fun-loving Professor Behrens overheard their conversation. He made a few amusing remarks and gave them some practical suggestions that started the boys in pursuit of a bright idea.

That afternoon the two buddies again walked the five miles to Bozeman and spent nearly their last dime to buy a pound of Limburger cheese. In the evening, when all the students were attending the Christmas program, the two boys planned their revenge.

But two of the huskiest girls, anticipating their move, had locked and barricaded all the dorm doors. The boys prowled until they discovered one door with hinge pins on the outside. By removing the pins they were able to get the door off. They entered the building through the kitchen and found their way to the girls' living quarters.

The two girls who were guarding the rooms gave away the identity of the guilty ones. Consequently, the rooms of the pranksters received the Limburger cheese—smeared on the radiators and placed in light sockets. When the heat and lights were turned on, the strong Limburger aroma saturated the building; and many days passed before the sickening smell vanished. Following that evening's activities, the principal put a stop to further retaliations.

The coldest weather of 1929 came in January, when the thermometer dropped to forty below zero. One afternoon during his second year as fireman Cliff went on shift in the boiler room and found his two fellow firemen and one of the teachers frantically working on the water pump for the steam boiler. They simply could not get it to work. No water level registered on the boiler's gauge.

Cliff felt uneasy and began investigating to see if the old boiler held any water at all. Opening the petcock below the water gauge he found no water there. More searching showed the boiler completely dry and only a little steam pressure left in it.

He quickly raked the live coals from the firebox, exclaiming, "You can thank the Lord you couldn't get that pump to work. There's not a bit of water in this boiler."

"How do you know that?" Professor Behrens asked.

Cliff opened the doors to the flues. Little jets of steam whistled through the leaking pipes, and this quickly explained where the water had gone. The untimely failure of the water pump thus averted a most certain explosion.

With forty-below-zero weather, the failure of the school's boiler posed a serious problem. Without heat or steam power they had no way to run the electric generator or the domestic water pump. Suddenly they were without heat, electricity, and water. All available help went to work to meet the emergency. Temporary stoves were set up in the dormitories, and outside toilets were made available.

A boilermaker came from Bozeman and installed three new flues and repaired the others. Although students kept the stoves going day and night, many water pipes froze and broke. Classes were curtailed, and some were simply discontinued until necessary repairs were made.

When the boilermaker finished his job at last and picked up his tools to leave, Cliff climbed the ladder to the top of the boiler and unscrewed the safety valve. Professor Behrens handed him a large funnel, which he placed in the opening. Then the professor went out to summon several boys to form a bucket brigade and fill the boiler.

While he waited in the dimly lighted boiler room, Cliff remembered his open schoolbooks on the old desk by the well. He climbed down, intending to put them away and close the desk. In the semidarkness he didn't notice the cover over the well was already removed. Without warning, he stepped over the edge.

He saved himself from going to the bottom by flinging out his arms. Shaking with fright and cold, he pulled himself up out of the well's mouth and climbed back up to the boiler. Soon the other boys arrived and passed buckets of water to him, which he poured into the funnel until the boiler was filled to the proper level.

At the time he felt no pain from his fall into the well, and as soon as his job with the boiler was finished he ran up to his room to change his shoes and socks. His feet felt cold and wet, he thought, from water spilled while handling the countless buckets. But—horrified—he saw his shoes streaked with blood and his socks a crimson color.

He made his way quickly to the office of the dean, whose wife was a nurse, and asked if his wounds could be bandaged. When he pulled his pant legs up he saw that long slices of flesh were peeled from the shinbones of both legs.

Professor Lansing quickly put him into his car and headed for the doctor's office in town.

5-R.T.P.

But before they arrived in Bozeman, the initial numbness left his legs, and Cliff could hardly endure the pain.

Although his legs were in bandages for several weeks, Cliff did his work and studies the best he could despite the soreness and stiffness that resulted from his fall.

The icy grip of a Montana winter finally gave way to warm spring weather, and in May the school term ended. Many fond farewells were said as the students returned to their homes scattered throughout the state. Although Cliff was not able to take full schoolwork, he had been successful in making his own way. C. B. Behrens, newly appointed academy principal, asked Cliff and Floyd if they would stay on for a couple of weeks after the school term ended to assist him in making some changes in the school plant. He held a little conference with Cliff.

"Why don't you stay and work this summer?" Professor Behrens asked. "You'll have money for the next school term, and you won't have to work so much after classes begin."

Cliff realized he gave good counsel, and he appreciated it, but he felt an obligation to his father, who needed him at home.

He worked hard that summer, helping to get the mill set up in a new location near good timber. But things did not go as expected. For the first part of the summer no cash came in, and Cliff received no wages. The last part of the summer he hauled slabs from another mill and sold them to a cheese factory for fuel. This brought in enough funds for the family to live on. But when fall came, again Cliff had no money for school; so he made plans to work his way through another year.

On the first three days of the school term, the students and faculty took a tour of Yellowstone National Park. Cliff accepted the invitation to drive one of the school cars through the park. This earned him ten dollars, and with this in his pocket he started another school year.

About midterm in the 1929-1930 school year, the old injuries on the front of his legs began giving him trouble. Although the wounds were healed over, sores developed on both legs. He treated them himself for a time, but finally he was forced to see a doctor.

He made several trips to a doctor's office for treatment, but his legs showed no improvement. The doctor, very concerned, asked, "How long have you been having trouble with your legs?"

"I had an accident about a year ago," Cliff answered. "A doctor treated them then, and they healed over. I thought they were all right when I came back to school last fall, but now these sores have developed over the old injuries."

More treatments followed, but inflammation began appearing on other parts of his body.

"Young man," the doctor advised, "I need to admit you to a hospital and administer some further tests and treatments. This is a form of blood poisoning, and if it is not treated promptly, you run the risk of losing your right leg."

Cliff was frightened. He did not have the money for the hospital expenses. After thinking further about his situation, he decided to go home. If there was danger of losing his leg, he wanted to see his family doctor at Hamilton, a man in whom he had great confidence. He took his problem to the academy principal and asked to be permitted to leave school for a time until he could get proper medical help.

"The problem is not that serious, is it, Clifford?" Professor Behrens questioned. "Did the doctor actually say there was a danger of losing your leg?"

"He wanted to put me in the hospital for treatment," Cliff replied. "He said I have a form of blood poisoning and if it is not properly treated, I stand a good chance of losing my leg. These sores are getting worse," he added, "and inflammations are showing up at other places on my body."

Behrens telephoned the doctor for a brief consultation. After the conversation Cliff wondered what the doctor said that made the principal seen so worried. Instead of giving Cliff permission to go home, Behrens asked him to wait at the school until he consulted with some other parties about the situation.

Before classes convened the next morning, H. C. Klement and Professor Behrens came to Clifford and revealed their decision.

"Clifford, since your accident occurred while you were working here, we feel it is our responsibility to provide you with medical care. We would like to send you to Missoula to see either Dr. Will or Dr. Charles Thornton. If you're willing, we'll make the arrangements and pay the expenses."

With a sigh of relief Cliff accepted the offer. Besides receiving the medical treatment he needed, he had an opportunity to visit at home, for Missoula was only about fifty miles from Hamilton.

So Cliff traveled to Missoula one day in January to receive the recommended treatments. They were simple but effective, and in a short time his injuries healed.

It was late in the day when he left the medical clinic. A bus line ran from Missoula to Hamilton, and he felt sure he could find a ride from Hamilton to home. His folks had no telephone and did not know he was coming, and he knew it would be long after dark by the time he could get home.

After the bus dropped him off at Hamilton, the end of its run, he caught a ride with a man going up the valley. He rode as far as the junction near Conner, where the man turned off the East Fork Road.

With three miles yet to travel and darkness overtaking him, Cliff trudged up the road toward home. A little snow began to fall, but he gave it scarcely a thought in his eagerness to see his family. But in a few minutes the storm became furious, and in the dark he could not tell where he was going. He tried to feel with his feet for the hard-packed tracks on the road, fearing that at any moment he would step off the steep roadbank and fall, in an avalanche of snow, into the icy creek just below. The wind increased; and Cliff, in his thin suit coat, felt as if he were locked in an ice factory.

Around midnight he lost all sense of direction but stumbled on, hoping to find and follow a fence line which might lead to a gate or a cattle guard near someone's house. Had he gone beyond the fence range? he kept asking himself. He well knew the vastness of the wide open range and could picture his fate as he wandered out there in the storm.

As he struggled along in the darkness, he suddenly felt an animal's nose against his leg. He whirled around, not knowing what might be attacking him. Then with a sigh of relief he saw it was old Bob, the family dog, jumping up and down with excitement.

Some people say dogs have a sixth sense, and indeed this may be true, for Bob, seemingly guided by a knowledge beyond comprehension, came to Cliff's rescue. Because the night was so stormy and cold, Cliff's father had taken pity on the dog and let him come into the house for the night. But near midnight Bob had begun to howl. Someone got out of bed and let him outdoors. Whimpering and with his nose to the ground, he darted out into the gloomy night.

Cliff had welcomed the dog's companionship many times before, but never so much as at this time of need.

Montana Snakes
and Broncs

Unfortunately (or as it seemed at the time), Cliff missed so much school and fell so far behind in his classwork that he dropped out for the remainder of the year. Again he helped his father in the mill near Medicine Tree, firing the steam engine, hauling lumber, and piling it.

Because it was something he *really* wanted to do, Cliff kept up a steady correspondence with a certain girl at Mount Ellis. He even tried his poetic bent by composing little poems to close each letter.

But through a friend he found out she had been two-timing him ever since he left the academy. Disappointed and hurt, he wrote a final letter to her, with an unusually long poem at the end:

> I built a fire with your letters
> And watched the flames leap high,
> 'Til at last they turned to ashes,
> Leaving only memories . . . bittersweet.

For a time Cliff nursed his injured feelings, but gradually the hurt healed.

The following spring the bottom dropped out of the lumber market, and many other lines of business also suffered. The milling company for which Cliff's father cut timber suspended operations.

One of the partners in the company stopped by the cookhouse one evening to chat a while. In the course of the conversation he made the remark, "There are twenty men for every job." A little while after he left, Cliff's youngest brother, Wayne, sent on his regular chore to fill the woodbox for the morning fire, struggled through the door with a big armload of wood. He dropped it into the box with a crash and remarked loudly, "I haven't seen any twenty men after *my* job."

By the first of May, seven months after the Wall Street stock-market crash, even the remote Bitterroot Valley felt the pinch of unemployment. Cliff expected to return to school by the following fall, but the depression and lack of work about concluded his plans for that year. The best prospect at the time was a few more days' work at a sawmill a couple of miles from home. Approaching his twentieth birthday, he felt that any further delay in completing his secondary education would be most embarrassing. Who wanted to go back to school at his age?

Just as things were looking hopeless, Cliff received a letter from his brother Floyd at Mount Ellis Academy, asking if he would be interested in working on a ranch in eastern Montana. Would he be interested! Would a drowning man be interested in a rope thrown to him? With sawmills closing down and men out of work everwhere, a job on a ranch looked like a dream come true. There might even be some horses to break, he thought with a new enthusiasm. And—interestingly—he learned that the rancher had two nice-looking daughters. Always interested in new ventures, he quickly accepted the offer.

Floyd purchased an old Model T Ford at Bozeman and planned to drive to a territory south of Miles City, where he was to sell books. Cliff planned to ride with his brother out to his ranch job. With school dismissed for the summer, a student by the name of Johnny, whose home lay in the same area south of Miles City, elected to ride along with the brothers. As soon as the old flivver was greased and repaired, the boys stowed their gear in the back seat and shimmied off.

They expected to drive the three-hundred-plus miles in a couple of days, but as the poet Robert Burns wrote, "The best laid schemes o' mice and men—" A few miles out of the village of Big Timber, a knock developed in the engine. A check of the oil level showed the Ford was nearly out of oil. Then Floyd discovered a missing bolt from the oil pan. The fellows succeeded in finding a replacement, but the threads were stripped.

Cliff whittled a plug with his pocketknife and hammered it into the hole. After the pan was filled with fresh oil, they managed to baby the old car into Billings, where they replaced its worn bearings.

When they finally arrived at Johnny's place, Floyd made a deal with the rancher to use one of his horses and a saddle part of the time during his canvassing rounds, to save money on transportation. The truth was that the brothers had already spent nearly all their money just getting into eastern Montana.

The "well-broke horse" Floyd borrowed proved to give him more ride than he expected. Cliff noted the way the big black mare humped her back and surmised that the ranch hands were about to enact one of the practical jokes that cowboys are noted for whenever they deal with unsuspecting greenhorns. But Floyd wasn't exactly a greenhorn.

"I'll hold her till you get set," Cliff suggested. He took a firm hold on the horse's bit. As soon as Floyd nodded, Cliff let go and jumped back.

She went up like a geyser and landed with both front legs stiff. Within the next minute or two she put on quite a show, all to the amusement of the men who were loitering around the corral. The big mare seemed intent on giving her rider a good pounding on the seat, but Floyd managed to stay with her. Finally, she raised her head and cantered off, recognizing who was master.

Floyd canvassed in his territory for a couple of days; then early Saturday morning he and Cliff told their friends goodbye and started off for the Gorsch ranch, where Cliff was to work. They made an early start, expecting to arrive in time for Sabbath School and church, as Cliff recalled that the little group of believers there held their services in the afternoon.

They had driven only a short way, however, when the dark clouds rolled in and a steady rain began to fall. The Ford had no top, and soon the boys' Sabbath clothes were soaked. The road became more and more slick as the dusty surface turned to mud. The car's smooth tires lost traction, and the boys were forced to put the tire chains on. One pushed while the other tried to drive. When they arrived at the ranch, they looked as though they had come too close to one of Yellowstone's mud geysers.

The Gorsches were expecting them and didn't seem surprised to see two mud-plastered young men in a mud-colored Ford pull into their yard about four o'clock Sabbath afternoon—wet, cold, and hungry.

Although they resembled drowned rats, their embarrassment disappeared with the warm reception. Gorsch, a gray-haired, rather stocky man with a pleasant manner and a friendly smile, met them at the door and introduced his family. Dry clothes were found for the boys, and soon they felt much more comfortable.

"I'll guess you haven't had a thing to eat all day," Mrs. Gorsch exclaimed. "Sarah and Dortha, will you help me get something for these boys to eat?"

The good meal and the warmth of the comfortable ranch house replaced the lingering chill of cold rain and blustering wind that Floyd and Cliff had endured that day. Gorch's easy manners and hearty laugh put the boys completely at ease.

"Now, don't you fellows bother about that 'Mr. Gorsch' stuff," his strong voice boomed. "Neighbors and friends just call me Jess."

Cliff's new job started early the next morning. He harnessed the team for the day's work and helped the girls with the milking. While they were eating breakfast, Floyd told of the "gentle" horse he rode on his canvassing circuit for a couple of days. They laughed in understanding.

"That's an old cowboy trick," Jess chuckled. "They'll do it every time they think they have a sucker."

Before they went their various ways for the day's work, Sarah picked up the book they used for family worship and began to read. She read from the well-worn copy of *Christ's Object Lessons* about the sower who went forth to sow. Cliff thought the words very appropriate. The story drew such a timely lesson from the springtime of the year. Jess closed his eyes and prayed for the group and their activities of the day.

A cold rain fell as Jess took Cliff out to the field to get him started at the plowing. Six horses were harnessed for his team: five of them were broncs and the sixth a well-broken old mare.

Cliff drove the horses when he worked his uncle's fields. He would sometimes introduce one unbroken horse into the string, but hitching *five* of them in a string of six seemed to Cliff to mean certain trouble.

"They don't savvy much yet," Jess stated, handing Cliff the lines. "That bald-faced bronc, the one in the furrow, is just plain mean. If old Baldy gets to actin' up, just lay into 'im with the whip, and he'll line up."

After one round in the field of about forty acres, Cliff found that the horses seemed to settle down and plow with ease. But while making the second round, the bald-faced bronc in the furrow suddenly stopped.

Cliff gave a crack with the whip. Just as the

whip struck the horse's rump, he saw why the horse had stopped. Lying there right in front of Baldy, a large rattlesnake coiled and began to rattle.

With the sting of the whip to urge him on, Baldy gave a gigantic leap right over the snake. As Cliff drew up the reins and yelled "Whoa!" the team stopped, with the seat of the plow—on which Cliff sat—directly over the snake. Fortunately, the low temperature that day made the snake very sluggish. Cliff plowed out three more diamondback rattlers the same day, each lying in a burrow close to the surface of the ground, waiting for fairer weather and warm sunshine.

Gone were the days of the great cattle kings who owned thousands of head of cattle. Jess, a relatively small operator, struggled to make a living on 300 acres of deeded land and his allotted government free range. Along with his livestock he raised hay, grain, and certified alfalfa seed.

"A rancher's sure gotta use his head these days," Jess observed one evening after supper. "Cattle and horses aren't worth much; wheat's 25 cents a bushel. But I get a good price for my seed alfalfa. I cut the first crop for hay and let the second go to seed. Then I thresh it," he explained. "After it's threshed, it still makes good feed for the stock, and I sell the seed for a profit."

Aware that age was creeping up on him, Jess explained to Cliff how he wanted a younger man to help rebuild his corrals and break new horses.

"I can't ride like I used to," he admitted. "Most of the neighbors use tractors and trucks for their work, but I don't savvy them machines, and I'm too old to change." Then Jess continued to give Cliff a rundown of his summer's work.

"There's fifteen head of good horses out there on the range that I need to get in and break for work on the place. My saddle horses are all getting old, except that sorrel mare I ride most of the time.

"Out on the range," Jess continued, "I've got a dandy four-year-old bay that's never had a saddle on 'im. I've waited so long now that most of the wild bunch are too old to make good saddle horses, but I think he's got possibilities.

"And just as soon as that bunch you're plowing with are gentled down tolerably, I want you to help me break that big buckskin gelding. I need to use him on one of the mowing machines this summer."

As Cliff continued with the plowing and the stretch of unplowed land became smaller, he thought about the day they would bring in the wild bunch. Of all the jobs on the ranch, his favorite was working with horses. When he finished the plowing, some of the alfalfa was ready to be cut; and Jess immediately started on the horse breaking, determined to use the big buckskin on the mower.

With the morning chores done one day, Cliff and Dortha saddled two of the best horses and headed toward the open range to find the wild bunch. With the help of the two ranch dogs, the horses were rounded up and came pell-mell down the lane toward the corral in a big cloud of yellow dust. As soon as the corral gate was closed behind the horses, Dortha went to the field where her father was mowing and took his place with the team. Jess rode up to meet Cliff at the corral.

"You'd better rope 'im," Jess called out, pointing to the bay he wanted broken to ride. "We'll put 'im in the other corral before we start on the buckskin."

The horses sensed the excitement and began to circle like trained animals in a circus arena. Cliff twirled the loop on his rope and cast. The noose fell past half a dozen noses and settled over the head of the bay. Quickly Cliff took a dally around the snubbing post in the center of the corral.

The bay snorted and lunged, but it was a losing battle. He submitted at last to a strong halter. His lead rope was snubbed securely to the horn of Jess's saddle as his favorite riding horse led the way to the holding corral.

81

The wild horses were turned out of the corral, and Buck the buckskin was hitched to one of the wagons with Diamond, a faithful workhorse. Jess drove while Cliff, riding a saddle horse and holding a rope fastened to Buck's halter, stayed alongside to keep away from the fences and gullies.

Next Jess began breaking him to pull the mowing machine. At the first sound of the machinery behind him, Buck grew wide-eyed and took off like a scared rabbit.

Cliff worried about Jess, fighting to control the wild horse while bouncing along on the seat of the mowing machine. But Jess stayed with him, and after a few tense moments and a crazy pattern of swaths cut through the field, Buck began to learn what mowing was all about. Soon he settled down to the job of getting the hay cut.

With two machines whirring away in the hayfield, Cliff thought, it wouldn't be long before he would be breaking the bay to ride.

"Well, Cliff—think you can ride the bay today?" Jess asked one morning after breakfast.

"I can sure give it a good try," Cliff responded, grinning widely.

He had looked forward to that day with great anticipation. As they neared the corral, where the horses stood haltered and ready, he noted with admiration the powerful, sleek animal—there was a touch of fire in his eyes.

Blazer, Cliff named him, noting the white stripe down his face.

Before Cliff was permitted to mount, the bay was rigged so that he could not get his head down to buck. Jess put a war bridle on him. By riding another horse in front, he could pull the bay down if he tried to rear up and fall over backward.

When all was in readiness, Cliff mounted and rode Blazer for a few yards. But as soon as the horse discovered he couldn't buck or rear backwards, he just lay down and sulked. Then a crack or two with the whip prompted him to spring to his feet, with Cliff still on his back.

Cliff rode the bay rigged that way for a couple of days, but secretly he didn't trust a horse broken in that manner. Out on the range alone one day, he decided to give the horse a chance. He unfastened the rope which prevented him from getting his head down.

When the blaze-faced horse suddenly discovered his new freedom, he humped his back, and the bucking show was on, with only a few stray head of cattle to watch. After Blazer decided that the rider was there to stay, he gave up and began learning the business of being a saddle horse.

After the first crop of alfalfa was cut, racked, and shocked, it was stacked to preserve it for winter's feeding. Cliff wasn't too surprised when the two strong Gorsch girls stepped in and did the work of two men in the field. But he was astonished when he saw frail-looking Mrs. Gorsch waiting at the stackyard, pitchfork in hand, ready to stack the first load.

"Poor people have poor ways," Jess explained. "We can't afford buckrakes and over-shot stackers, but we get the work done. Come winter, the stock don't seem to mind how the hay was stacked."

In addition to stacking the hay, Mrs. Gorsch and the girls prepared all the meals and washed the dishes. Cliff felt sympathetic, seeing the women working so hard. He always helped with the dishes and, when possible, helped to prepare the vegetables.

In the heat of the summer the rattlesnakes seemed to think that hay shocks were made for their comfort and convenience. Many snakes were discovered when the shocks were loaded on the wagon, and they were routinely killed, as in other years. But they still seemed to abound.

One day while putting the last shocks on a loaded wagon, a rattler slithered right down Cliff's fork handle. He let go of the tool as if it were hot and jumped back. It seemed almost a miracle to him that no one had suffered a snakebite that summer.

The Gorsch family made plans to attend the

Seventh-day Adventist camp meeting held that summer at Billings. Sarah, the oldest daughter, also needed a tonsillectomy. Their family doctor recommended that it be performed in Billings. Jess asked if he would stay on the ranch and do the chores while they were away. Cliff readily accepted the task.

With the hay all cut and stacked, the only chores to do would be to milk the cows, separate the milk and wash the cream separator every day, take care of the cream, and feed and water the chickens. It sounded to Cliff like an easy job.

What would he do with all his extra time? he wondered. He decided that since he would have time on his hands, he would break another horse to ride. He could be riding after the cows on a new horse when the family returned.

Not considering the possibility that he might get hurt and that nobody else was around for miles, Cliff rounded up several horses off the range, picked out a nice gelding, and roped him. After haltering the bronc and making him secure, he turned the others out.

He saddled and bridled the horse, rigged up a blindfold, and mounted. When securely seated, he pulled the blindfold from the horse's eyes. No one but the two ranch dogs and the old Tabby cat were there to see the show, but Cliff was sure it was a good one. He managed to keep his seat and rode the big horse to the finish.

But a couple of days later, while coming down a little ridge, the horse got his head down and without warning began bucking again. Cliff rode until they came to the base of the hill. There a barbed wire fence ran directly across the course the horse was taking.

Rather than get tangled up in the fence with a bucking horse, Cliff decided to jump. Just as he loosened his grip to jump, the horse whirled around and went parallel with the fenceline, throwing Cliff right through the fence between two strands of wire. He landed with a whump in a bed of prickly-pear cactus.

When the Gorsch family returned, however, Cliff rode up proudly on a newly broken horse. But instead of smiles of approval as he had expected, a look of consternation came over Jess's face.

It seemed that Mrs. Gorsch had worried all the time they were gone, fearing that Cliff would try just such a thing. She knew no one was near to help him if he were injured.

Nothing was said about it; so Cliff put the horse in the corral and helped unload the car.

"I was so afraid you would do something like that, Clifford," Mrs. Gorsch said later. "I am so thankful you didn't get hurt."

In a few days Floyd showed up at the ranch

unexpectedly, with his conference colporteur field secretary. The two seemed determined that Cliff should spend the rest of his summer selling books.

"Why, I'm no book salesman," Cliff insisted. "I couldn't sell books."

"How do you know?" Floyd argued. "If I can do it, there is no reason why you can't. Besides, Gorsches don't need you now. The work is all caught up, and these good people can't afford to pay you wages when they really don't need you."

Finally Cliff consented to give bookselling a try. Little did he know what adventures lay ahead.

"We've Got Thirty-Two Guns"

The two brothers agreed, before they started canvassing, that Floyd would use the Model T and Cliff a saddle horse while working their territory near the town of Ekalaka. Jess offered Cliff the use of a horse and saddle, and he accepted.

"That white Indian pony I'm loaning you is tough as nails, Cliff," Jess commented. "If you cut across country, you can likely beat Floyd to where you're a going."

Carefully setting the directions in his mind, Cliff started out early in the morning. Floyd, with the luggage stowed in the back of the Ford, drove away at about the same time. Although the car was able to travel much faster, the distance to Ekalaka by road was much farther than the route Cliff planned to take.

The fellows arranged to meet in front of the courthouse in Ekalaka. Then they would look for a place near town to make their headquarters while selling books in the area.

Floyd stopped to fill the Ford at a gas pump in front of a little country store. Just as he was driving away, Cliff came jogging along on his horse. Floyd waved him over to the side of the road, where they held a little conference.

"I didn't get a chance to talk to you alone before we left the ranch," Floyd said.

Cliff looked at him inquiringly.

"I think that meeting people and talking to them about Christianity will do more for you than a college Bible course," he continued earnestly. "It will bring you close to the Lord, Cliff. In fact, you can't expect to succeed in this work unless you have God's help."

"I can believe that, all right," Cliff replied skeptically. "I'll need the Lord's help if I sell any books at all. But as it is, I'm not too sure about my standing with the Almighty."

"God can use you," Floyd encouraged, "if you're willing to yield your life to him to be used to help others. But your life has to be a testimony of your faith. If you don't live your faith, people will see right through you and conclude that you don't believe what you're saying."

With those thoughts uppermost in his mind, Cliff rode away into what he felt was a most uncertain future. Other thoughts wove their way in and out of his mind—the Gorsch family—such devoted people those folks were. He had looked forward to the devotional period they held at the beginning of each day. And largely because of these solemn moments each morning, Christianity had begun to take on a new dimension in his life. His former opinions and prejudices all but vanished, and almost unconsciously his attitude changed. He felt a desire to know the warm love of Jesus Christ in his heart.

Cliff found plenty of time for quiet thinking on his lonely journey over miles of uninhabited land. There seemed to be an abundance of game—prairie chickens, antelope, deer, and of course, jackrabbits. Several times he rode through large villages of prairie dogs. The sun rose hot over eastern Montana as Cliff rode on and on in a bleak no-man's-land.

"If I could just find a spring of decent water," he murmured, half aloud. All there seemed to be was alkali water. The sulfur in it made it smell like spoiled eggs.

His thoughts rambled on as he talked to himself.

"I don't see why the settlers fought with the Indians over this barren country. Old Red Cloud said it belonged to his people, and I say they were welcome to it. Guess that was back in the days when Grandpa began scouting for the army with Jim Bridger."

All those things had happened before the army decided to build a fort that was nearly destoyed by the Indians, Grandpa had once told him. That was the time, Cliff remembered, that Portugee Phillips had made his historic ride to Fort Laramie in sub-zero weather with a message for help. Cliff wished he could have a little of that coolness just now in the scorching July heat.

He recalled the various events of Northwest history as he had heard them repeated by old-timers as they sat around the cookhouse on his grandfather's ranch at Bozeman. And what would he have done, he wondered to himself, in a situation like his great-uncle Elliot faced the time he spent a night with road agents in one of their hangouts near Virginia City.

As the sun began to set, Cliff could see the outline of a windmill on the horizon, and he thought he saw the outline of a water tank. The pony he rode apparently sensed it also and quickened his step. In the lingering twilight Cliff rode past a corral to an overflowing tank. A gentle breeze turned the windmill, and cool water poured from the pump. Nothing had ever looked and tasted so good to Cliff. As the horse drank from the tank, Cliff had his fill right from the waterspout.

He rode up to the ranch house and knocked at the door. No response. He looked around for some sign of life. A calico cat rubbed against his leg. Nothing else stirred, except his empty stomach. He had hoped to spend the night there, but a strange, eerie feeling suddenly crept over him, and he wanted to get away.

He remounted and rode off into the gathering darkness.

He had traveled for an hour or more when his horse turned off the road abruptly and stopped. This must be a road off to some ranch, Cliff thought, straining his eyes in the darkness. He saw a wire gate nearby, opened it without dismounting, and rode through. He closed it and gave the horse free rein.

Suddenly a pack of vicious dogs surrounded him, barking and growling. The hair on their backs bristled.

The disturbance woke some men in their bedrolls on the ground nearby, and they called the dogs back. A man about Cliff's size and age got up and lit a lantern.

"How in the world did you get in here without the dogs eating you up? Old Dutch never allows anybody inside the fence."

"I just opened the gate and rode in," Cliff answered with a shrug. "The dogs didn't bother me till I stopped."

The young man led him over to a corral, where the pony was unsaddled and turned loose for the night.

"I came to a place about an hour back," Cliff ventured. "There didn't seem to be anyone around, so I came on. I'm headed for

Ekalaka," he explained, "where I'm to meet my brother."

"That would be the Clare Thomas place." The young fellow paused. "He got shot the other day, so he ain't around no more." A few more moments passed before he spoke again.

"I'm Ed Dexter. That's my dad and my brother Lew," he said, nodding his head toward the other men. "We're puttin' up hay here on the homestead."

"I'm Cliff Rouse." The two men shook hands as Cliff spoke. Ed led him into the old building—probably the homestead shack, Cliff thought.

"There's been a lot of killin's around here lately," Ed said quietly.

"What seems to be the trouble?" Cliff asked.

"Oh, one thing and another." Ed paused. "Our neighbors to the north of us got into a fight over one of 'em runnin' sheep on the other fellow's range and eatin' off the grass to where the cattle didn't have no chance. They got into a fight over it, and one of 'em got shot."

While he was talking, another man stepped into the shack.

"This here's my brother Lew," Ed stated. After the two shook hands, Lew crouched in typical cowboy fashion as Ed continued.

"They've been havin' a regular cattle and

sheep war over free government range a few miles from here. But this here Clare Thomas deal is somethin' else."

He didn't go on to explain, and Cliff felt it was none of his business to ask questions. Ed's face suddenly clouded, as if a storm were passing through his mind.

"They got Clare Thomas, but they're not gonna get us," he growled. Cliff sensed the tense atmosphere in the old cabin. Lew crouched on the other side of the room like an eagle ready to swoop down upon its prey.

"We've got thirty-two guns here in this house," Ed continued, looking squint-eyed at Cliff. "They're all loaded, and we'll empty every one of 'em before those guys can get us."

Just then a heavy-set man with shaggy gray hair entered the shack. His face bore the same hard scowl of the younger men. As Cliff watched the old man, he noted how his arms and shoulders twitched. His hands shook nervously, and he walked with a jerking movement.

"This is Dad." Ed nodded toward the man who had just entered the room.

The old man said nothing, but walked over to a little stand near where Cliff sat. Opening a drawer, he reached in and drew out a revolver. Turning toward Cliff, he spoke for the first time.

"They thought they got the gun that killed

Clare Thomas," the old man quavered, "but there it is, right there." He leveled the gun barrel right under Cliff's nose.

Cliff stared straight into the barrel of the big forty-five. It looked to him as big as a cannon. He felt he didn't dare show fear. He kept a steady gaze on the man who held the weapon.

Then the old man replaced the revolver, closed the drawer, and walked out of the shack without saying another word.

After a moment Lew took up the conversation.

"You can't make it to Ekalaka tonight. You can stay here with us, and I'll show you the way in the morning."

"If I'd only brought a bedroll with me," Cliff mused. "I wished I had thought of it."

Lew and Ed held a little conference and decided that their father had the most room in his bedroll.

"You can sleep with Dad. He's got a wide bedroll."

Clifford strolled over to where old Dexter lay. Still awake, he moved over, and Cliff crawled in.

What kind of a jackpot have I gotten into now! Cliff wondered as he lay quietly. If he tried to get up and slip away, the dogs would be right upon him. The safest course would be to stay put until morning. He was very tired after the long day's ride and fell asleep.

"Come and get it, or I'll throw it out!" old Dexter shouted from the door of the shack. Cliff woke with a start. Where in the world was he, and what was all the shouting about?

"Come and get it, or I'll throw it *out*!" the old man bellowed again. Cliff noticed that the sun was already about an hour high. He dressed quickly and made his way toward the shack as the two younger Dexters came in from the hayfield.

Cliff took special pains to avoid any mention of the Clare Thomas tragedy or the discussion of the night before. The three young men took turns washing up and then sat down around the rough table. Dexter took a huge pan of biscuits from the oven, and as soon as they were seated, he took up the bacon and eggs and poured the coffee.

Cliff didn't eat bacon or drink coffee. He hesitated as he looked over the meal.

"Dig in, kid," the old man invited. "We ain't got nothing fancy, but you're sure welcome to what we've got."

All the tension and bitterness of the evening before disappeared as everyone went out of his way to be friendly. Lew and Ed conversed with Cliff like old-time friends, and even the dogs seemed to accept him.

Cliff stayed by after the meal to help Dexter clear the table and wash the dishes. The food scraps, including a sizable stack of biscuits, were set out for the dogs. Old Dutch, a huge animal—half Russian wolfhound and half greyhound—charged in at the mention of his name. The old man began tossing him the biscuits, the dog gulping them as he came. He didn't miss a single one.

Cliff started for the corral to get his horse. As he saddled the Indian pony, Ed came over and examined the brand.

"Never saw that brand before. Whose is it?"

I really don't know," Cliff answered. "It isn't the brand of the man who owns him. He bought this horse or traded for it, I think he said. He's a tough one. I rode him from about fifteen miles northwest of Broadus to here yesterday."

"That would be—well, right at seventy-five miles, give or take a little," Ed figured, whistling under his breath.

"I felt like it must have been at least a hundred when I got here last night," Cliff said with a chuckle.

Cliff walked to where the men worked in the hayfield and thanked them for their hospitality. Lew stuck his fork into a stock of hay and volunteered to accompany Cliff to the top of the hill so he could point the way to Ekalaka.

"Down there about a half mile you'll run into a road," he directed. "Just follow it east, and it'll lead you to town. It's about fifteen miles. And if you ever come by this way again," he added, "stop in and see us."

Cliff rode on toward Ekalaka, wondering at the change in attitude at the Dexter ranch. Did he imagine it? Or could it be that the Lord had heard his silent petition when he retired for the night? He had claimed the promise of Psalm 34:4, "I sought the Lord, and he heard me, and delivered me from all my fears."

Just fifteen more miles, Cliff thought, as he struck out along the road young Dexter told him about. "I'll bet Floyd will be worried about me, thinking I'm lost out here somewhere." Cliff spoke out loud, and the pony flipped his ears back to listen.

When he rode into town, he could find no trace of Floyd.

"A stranger in a Model T with a number six Gallatin County license?" the garage attendant repeated. "Nope, I'm sure he hasn't been here. You're the first stranger I've seen for at least a couple of days."

Then it was Cliff's turn to worry, Floyd had his bed, his clothes, and, above all, his bookselling prospectus. Cliff had no money, but with his prospectus he hoped he could make a sale and find a place to stay.

The attendant looked him over for a minute. "Are you in trouble?"

"Well, yes," Cliff admitted. My brother has my bed and clothes and the books I planned to sell."

"A book salesman, huh? What kind of books are you selling?"

"*The Home Physician*," Cliff informed him. "It's a kind of doctor book."

He proceeded to give the man a canvass. The man showed an interest and told him to go out to his house and tell his wife about it.

"We could sure use a doctor book at our house. I'll look out for your brother, and you can put your horse in the pasture." With a wave, he gave Cliff the directions to his place. How could he be so lucky! Cliff thought.

Floyd didn't show up for three days. Cliff knew he must be having trouble with the car. Just as he was wondering if he should ride out and begin searching, Floyd drove into town.

The brake bands on the old Ford had burned out, Floyd related, leaving him stranded in a ravine. A passing rancher had stopped to see if he could help. It seemed he knew of an abandoned ranch nearby where there was an old rubber belt. With his jackknife Floyd cut out the new brake bands and installed them. The improvised bands were not of the best quality, but he made it to Ekalaka with them.

Arrangements were made with the garage owner to exchange a doctor book for board and room while the fellows canvassed the town. They each sold a few books and then moved on to new territory.

Canvassing became more difficult the latter part of the summer. The nation's economic depression plus drought conditions in eastern Montana worked such hardships on some families that they were hard put even to supply food for their tables. Under such circumstances few people could afford to buy books.

Cliff's hopes for a scholarship at the academy faded with each passing day, but he realized that he had gained some valuable experience. His heart was warm, and he thrilled to tell others what a change had taken place in his life.

But one other problem still remained. For quite some time now, he had struggled with the habit of smoking cigarettes; and Cliff knew that God was not pleased as long as he smoked. Periodically he would throw away his cigarettes and declare it quits, but the craving would come back to mock him. Like the apostle Paul, he acknowledged "another law" warring against the law of his mind. Whenever he thought he had the habit whipped, he discovered he was not the master of his own will.

He had known, while still a boy in grade school, that in playing with tobacco he was headed in the wrong direction; but he felt certain he could quit before he really got the habit. But he found himself faced with a real battle when occasionally, with an active and miserable conscience, he would smoke with some of his buddies.

Later in the summer Cliff returned to the area near the Gorsch ranch to sell books. He had little success, for the same economic problem existed there as at Ekalaka. He contacted a rancher he knew, whose property bordered that of Jess Gorsch.

After Cliff finished his canvass, the neighbor said, "Cliff, I'll tell you what I'll do. I'll buy the book if you will help me get this alfalfa seed cut and threshed, and I'll pay you wages for the time you work. Is it a deal?"

The arrangement looked good to Cliff. He worked for two weeks and received cash wages, and with the sale of the book he had enough money to return to the academy and pay his entrance fee. And he was scheduled to work once again in the boiler room.

Returning to the academy in the autumn full of hope for the future, Cliff determined to obey the rules of the school, including the no-smoking rule.

Some new students, however, found it a problem to comply with that rule. And instead of taking a firm stand for the principles of Christian living, Cliff yielded to his weakness and secretly smoked with them. He felt condemned over his constant failure, and after a time he decided he could not honestly continue in such a pattern.

Discouraged and ashamed, Cliff decided to leave school. What would he do? Where would he go?

Buried Alive

Cliff had such good plans in the spring for the upcoming school year—he would make enough money during the summer to go to school and take a full load of classwork. He had wanted to finish his academy work that year and graduate. But, one by one, his plans had burst like soap bubbles.

As he made the decision to leave campus, discouraged and heartsick, he thought of the fellow with whom he had recently broken the school rules by smoking. The climax came when Delbert brought a cigar to the boiler room where Cliff worked the evening shift.

Together they smoked, and of course the strong smell of the cigar could not be stifled. Soon the principal came to investigate. As he opened the door, he saw Delbert puffing away.

In counseling with Delbert's father, the principal could not convince him that his son would do such a thing; and the man insisted that his son be allowed to remain in school.

As Cliff banked the fire in the boiler and closed down operations for the night, the principal entered the room and asked Cliff to do him a favor.

"Delbert's father will not believe me that his son was smoking. Will you come up and tell him that it is so? I hate to ask you to do this," he said apologetically, "but he thinks I am prejudiced and have made up this story. I need you to convince him that I am telling the truth."

The principal was like a father to Cliff and understood the situation; but he had no way of knowing that Cliff was also involved—not until Cliff walked into the room and told the men that both he and Delbert had been smoking.

Feeling that all his hopes were dashed, Cliff hated his weakness. Why did I ever start such a stupid habit in the first place? he asked himself. I had a really good experience last summer; now I am only a weakling. I tried to obey the rules, but—

Feeling he was too much of a man to cry, he bottled up his emotions, packed his clothes, and headed east.

On the way to Livingston he came upon a highway construction crew. The contractor on the job turned out to have been a neighbor of the Rouses when they had lived in Livingston.

When Cliff applied for work, he was hired at once.

If he had asked for the Sabbath off, perhaps he could have received this permission. But, discouraged as he was, he felt like a hypocrite even to ask. Already the words of 1 Corinthians 3:17 stood like a witness against him: "If any man defile the temple of God, him shall God destroy."

When Saturday morning came, Cliff went to work. He felt he was a defeated man. That morning several members of the Livingston Seventh-day Adventist Church were on their way to Mount Ellis Academy for the worship services. They drove past the construction site, and Cliff spotted them. He turned his back, hoping they would not recognize him. but they were delayed by the road equipment and stopped right beside him waiting for the road to be cleared. One of the ladies looked over and saw him.

"Why, there's Clifford Rouse!" she announced to the others. They all waved and smiled. Although certain he was thoroughly condemned, he tried to smile as he acknowledged their greeting.

In his discouragement Cliff may have turned away from God, but God had not turned away from him. From His great heart of love, God was about to show him the way to successful Christian living.

At the request of the school board, Cliff's father returned to Mount Ellis to install a second boiler in the powerhouse. When the job was completed, he leased some mining property up Trail Creek and began prospecting, expecting to open a coal mine.

When the road construction project near Livingston was completed, Cliff moved with his father to a shack on the leased property and began working with him in the mine. They pulled pillars in the old mine in order to have coal to sell while they relocated the vein and opened up the new mine. Every thirty feet in the old mine's tunnel a pillar was left for support while the miners took out the nearby coal. When these pillars were mined out, sometimes hundreds of tons of earth and rock would cave in, filling the vacancy. Pulling pillars was very dangerous work.

Cliff had barely begun his work in the mine one morning when he heard a faint cracking sound overhead. Instantly he was alert to danger. Already a big crack—large enough to put his arm into—had developed overhead. He dared not go directly under it. He took his miner's pick, stuck it in the crack, and gave it a little pull as he stood against the face of the vein of coal, which was on a forty-five degree angle. In positioning himself this way, the coal and rock would not fall on him, should there be a cave-in.

In the distance he could hear timbers cracking as they gave way to the weight of coal and rock. It sounded to Cliff as though the whole mine had caved in. He headed quickly for the nearest escape route—the air shaft—a small, sloping tunnel upward to the surface, which provided ventilation for the miners working far below. Cliff began scrambling up the shaft but soon realized the cave-in had triggered an avalanche of loose rock, which came tumbling down the shaft. A suffocating cloud of dust enveloped him as he dived back down into the mine and hid behind a protecting wall of rock. With a sickening rush of awareness he realized that his route out of the mine was blocked by the cave-in.

As he crouched against the mine wall, his heart racing with fear, he told himself to calm down and think through his predicament. He had his lunch, enough water to drink, and fuel for his carbide lamp for the day. But as he waited, his lamp began to dim, and he knew it would soon go out because of the lack of oxygen in the stuffy atmosphere. So he blew the light out, hoping to save enough oxygen to breathe.

He sat down on the cold mine floor and pondered his misfortune. The creeping oppression of total darkness pressed in on him. He knew his father and brother were working nearby, trying to dig enough coal to fill an order. Were they buried too? Would they get out of there alive or die from lack of oxygen or thirst? He sat dazed in the blackness, questioning whether he would ever again see the light of day.

Rousing himself, he took his pick and tapped three times on the mine wall. He waited a minute or two and tapped again. No answer. At intervals during the next few hours he repeated the tapping and listening, but no response came. What had happened to his father and Floyd? Would he ever know?

Cliff shivered even in the sultry darkness. A picture of his life-style passed before his eyes—how he had been thinking and behaving lately—and he realized that many of his ideas and actions were totally worthless. Yet he had an intense desire to live. Why was he so weak, so unstable, stumbling along from one day to the next? He felt he must ask God's forgiveness and get things squared up.

Suddenly the promise of 1 John 1:9 came to mind as it never had before: "If we confess our sins, he is faithful and just to forgive us our sins, and to cleanse us from all unrighteousness."

Hours dragged by. Cliff decided if he could only explain to God his pitiful weakness, perhaps he could get the help he needed. Buried alive—as it seemed—in the old mine tunnel, these matters of earnest import came to the forefront of his mind; and he prayed his first real prayer:

"Lord I'm such a miserable person. I don't even know how to pray like I ought to," he confessed. "I want to give You my heart, but I guess I don't really know how to give it. So just take it, Lord. You keep it for me; I can't keep it. And if I get out of here alive, will You always keep me? And—" He paused thoughtfully. "Oh, yes, Lord, if I get out of here alive, I want to serve You. Help me to serve You. Give me the strength I'll need to do whatever You want me to do. Amen."

At the close of his simple prayer, Cliff felt the warmth of a loving and forgiving God—a divine closeness he'd never before experienced. He thought he would even have the courage to go back to school, if that was God's plan for him. And with God at the helm of his life, he was sure he would be given strength to keep the school rules. He believed with all his heart that "I can do all things through Christ which strengtheneth me." Philippians 4:13.

More hours dragged on, but Clifford no longer felt the cold terror that had seized him when the mine caved in. A calmness came over him—a certain knowledge that whether he got out or not, God's way would be the best way.

As time passed endlessly, Cliff thought he heard one faint scrape of a shovel; but when he heard nothing more, he wondered if his imagination was tricking him. Sometime later, however, he heard the same sound again, more distinctly. He tapped again on the vein of coal. He shouted until he was hoarse. Silence. Apparently no one heard him.

But again, after a while, he was sure he heard the mumbling of voices. Or was it only in his mind? Then he recognized his father's voice. "I wonder if he is still alive."

"Yes!" Cliff yelled, nearly choking on the word.

In a few more minutes a shaft of yellow light broke through the darkness, and his father's head appeared over the pile of debris. The men worked steadily, and the opening was made large enough for Cliff to squeeze through—alive and unhurt!

That evening as he lay alone with his thoughts on his bed in the ramshackle cabin, his mind went over the day's events. He was tempted to think that he would have escaped the cave-in safely even if he hadn't prayed, but he had made a commitment to God, and he intended to keep that commitment. He didn't tell anyone of the new direction the course of his life had taken. He had failed before, trying to do things on his own, but this time he knew that with God's help he would succeed all the way.

It did take courage for Cliff to walk again up

to the administration building at Mount Ellis Academy. He felt ashamed to face Principal Hanson, wondering what he would think.

"Well, guess I'll soon find out." He took a deep breath, opened the front door, and stepped inside. A friendly smile from the secretary gave him courage.

"Come right in," she invited. "Mr. Hanson will be glad to see you."

Cliff's feet felt heavy as he followed her to the office doorway.

"Good morning, Clifford." Mr. Hanson stood to his feet and flashed a wide smile. His firm handshake encouraged Cliff and made him feel welcome. When Cliff told him of his new determination—that with God to help he knew he could keep the rules and not smoke—Mr. Hanson answered in a kindly way.

"Well, Cliff," he said softly, happiness shining in his eyes, "I have prayed for you every day you have been gone. The testimony you just gave is the one I have longed to hear."

From that day on, Cliff entered into the schedule of classes with new determination, and his grades took a decided upturn. But he was not allowed to take all the classes he needed in order to graduate. Well, he reasoned, it was probably better that way; it did give him time for some recreation. The change of pace was refreshing to him.

For one such period of recreation, the social committee planned a Sunday outing for the student body and the faculty members to tour a cave, now called the Lewis and Clark Caverns. Cliff drove his father's truck to provide some of the transportation. And—he hoped that a certain young lady would ride with him! But instead, one of the faculty members and his wife chose to ride along.

They parked the cars and trucks at the end of the road and followed a trail which led about a mile and a half back into the mountains to the entrance to the cave. A guide took them on a tour, which lasted an hour or more, to see the wonders of the vast underground cavern, much of which had not yet been explored.

Everyone enjoyed the day, which closed with a last bit of excitement. A rattlesnake alarmed the students as they hiked down the trail toward the cars. To Cliff and the other ranch boys a rattlesnake was nothing new, and they quickly dispatched the creature with rocks and sticks.

Graduation day brought big hopes for some of the students, but for Cliff it was a time for reflecting. One of the senior girls had stolen his heart, and when she left campus, Cliff felt she would take away the sunshine of their happy days together and he would be left alone with his heartache. Elizabeth would be going on to college. She had canvassed the previous two summers, and he assumed she would be doing the same the upcoming summer. But Elizabeth had other ideas.

Most of the academy farmland lay idle at the time, and some of Elizabeth's relatives, who raised potatoes near Livingston, offered to give her seed potatoes if she would rent the land and plant the crop. She was not a farm girl, and Cliff wondered how the arrangement would work out. If that was her decision, he thought, he would be delighted to help her all he could.

So he hauled her seed potatoes to Mount Ellis and helped her cut and plant them. Very soon after school closed for summer vaction, the ground was prepared and the potatoes planted.

One Saturday night during the early part of the summer, while the young people at Mount Ellis were playing games, Elizabeth fell and broke her ankle. This put an end to her work with the potato crop, but several of her classmates and friends came in and helped. Eagerly she looked forward to selling her potatoes and paying off her younger sister's bills at the academy. With what she had left she hoped to supplement her job at Walla Walla College and pay her expenses there.

Then Cliff turned to the problem of how to raise money for the next school year. His fa-

113

ther had sold his mine, and both Cliff and Floyd searched in vain for work. They took a few orders for coal, but there was very little profit in it. Living together in a little cabin at Chestnut, they were reduced to a diet of potatoes and beans.

Once during the summer, the brothers got a job hauling wheat. The price shot up to 27 cents a bushel, and a wheat farmer had decided to sell. He had stored his last two crops in granaries, and he sold it all at one time.

Cliff kept inquiring for work and was able to get a few farm jobs here and there. In the latter part of August and through September he worked hard in the local wheat harvest, hauling grain with his father's truck.

When Cliff returned to Mount Ellis for the fall term, he took the responsibility of getting Elizabeth's potato crop harvested. But, unfortunately, the price of potatoes that autumn dropped to an all-time low. She sold her crop to a merchant in Livingston for 50 cents a hundred—for number one potatoes! After the harvesters were paid and the bill at the academy settled, she had very little money left.

Hard luck seemed to dog her steps that autumn. The drugstore near Walla Walla College where she was promised employment changed hands, and the new owner did not need a girl to help in the store.

She applied for work at the college sanitarium, but the word came that it had been closed. The school board voted to purchase Walla Walla General Hospital in the city of Walla Walla, several miles from the college. But they provided no transportation for employees and were not taking student help at the time.

Elizabeth felt as if the world had suddenly turned against her—changes taking place at a dizzy rate. The elementary school enrollment at Mount Ellis suddenly mushroomed, and the teachers asked for an assistant. So the school board asked Elizabeth to take part of the students into another room and supervise them under the teacher's guidance. Of course she felt disappointed about missing college that year but gladly accepted the offer from the academy.

The change in her plans made Clifford happy.

"Next year we can go to college," he consoled her. "After all, I was afraid I'd lose you to some good-looking college student," he teased.

"Oh, nonsense," she replied, with a sly grin.

After two months the student enrollment eased at the elementary school, and funding declined so sharply that the school could no longer afford two teachers. Elizabeth's future seemed uncertain again.

Then another surprise developed in Elizabeth's life—Cliff proposed marriage. He truly wanted to make a home for her, he said, since she had no home of her own. Her mother had recently remarried and lived in California. But then Cliff was puzzled because Elizabeth seemed troubled and uncertain.

In the discussion which followed, Cliff learned of rumors going around concerning his past life. Elizabeth quietly confessed that two church officials had met with her just a few days earlier to dissuade her from making any such commitment to Cliff. Certain individuals warned that she was making a serious mistake by keeping company with him. The conclusion was that she would be throwing her life away on a "wild good-for-nothing." When Cliff heard this report, he stared at Elizabeth, too stunned for words. At last he spoke.

"Well, at least part of it is true," Cliff murmured softy. "I have been good for nothing, but I came back to school to try to make myself good for something—with God's help."

He gazed at the floor for a long minute, then heaved himself out of the chair. He turned toward the door, put his hand on the knob, and paused. This is it, he thought, the end of something good and precious. But he wanted Elizabeth to hear his final word.

"I have appreciated knowing you," Cliff

said, holding his chin up resolutely, "and I want you to know one thing. I want to be in the kingdom, and with God's help I will."

Suddenly Elizabeth ran to the door and leaned against it. She reached her hands out to him.

"That's all I need to know," she said earnestly, looking deep into his eyes, "and it's good enough for me."

On Thanksgiving Day, November 26, 1931, Elizabeth Martin and Clifford Rouse were married and went out to meet the challenges of life together. They both knew that a long and toilsome road lay ahead, but in the strength of God they faced the future with joy.

The Miracle Suit

The newlyweds rented a cozy upstairs apartment, and although their furnishings were meager, they were happy to manage with what they had.

"Now we have a home of our own." Cliff hugged his bride as they sat down to their first breakfast together.

"And we can make it the home that we've both longed for," Elizabeth added, her face glowing with joy. Each recalled the unhappiness and pain of their childhood homes, where the spirit of love between mother and father was largely absent and continual strife shook the family foundation.

For the remainder of the first winter, Cliff continued working in a nearby coal mine. The two prayed that the right opportunity would arise so they could move on toward completing their education. Nor did Cliff forget his commitment made at the cave-in of the old Meadow Creek mine.

"We should be doing something besides just marking time," Cliff remarked one evening. He wondered about the future and the steps to take toward it.

"It looks to me like you are doing something. You're directing the music for church," she reminded him. "After all, you have to learn to crawl before you can walk."

"Yes, I know," Cliff replied, "but I believe that music is a gift, and this kind of gift is of no value unless it is improved."

"You must be patient and wait for the Lord to give you the opportunity," his wife insisted.

Cliff sighed. "I suppose you're right. But surely there's something more to do than mining coal for a living."

"You could sell books."

"What? We'd starve to death for sure," Cliff groaned.

"Well—ask God about it," Elizabeth suggested.

"All right, but only if you are willing to get along on an uncertain income, and if it's what the Lord wants me to do."

Cliff knew he lacked faith, and he needed something to strengthen his courage.

"Lord, I know that the colporteur work is a good work," he prayed, alone with his thoughts that evening, "but I need encouragement. If this is what You want me to do, send me something proper to wear."

Cliff felt much better after he put the situation into the hands of the Lord. He was certain God would not bother with such a foolish prayer as a request for a suit of clothes. He really didn't want to sell books, but was afraid to say No.

The next day one of Elizabeth's girl friends dropped by to visit while Cliff was at the mine. During the conversation she suddenly said, "Do you think Clifford would be offended if I gave him a suit? My boss has a beautiful suit that he doesn't like, and he's going to give it away. I think it would just fit Clifford."

Thus before Cliff could think twice, he was the new owner of a handsome hand-tailored suit—and it was a perfect fit. Within the same week the colporteur field secretary called to ask if Cliff would go with him to a colporteur workshop to be held in Butte.

Overwhelmed by this sudden response to his reluctant prayer, Cliff knew he could not say No. When the colporteur institute was over, he launched out to make new discoveries in Christian sales work.

In later years he saw that his experiences in literature evangelism were of importance to him in many ways. He was truly grateful for the opportunity God had given him and the success he found as he made use of it.

Cliff hoped to start school at Walla Walla College the following autumn, but after settling his account with the Book and Bible House, funds for school were sadly lacking. But he knew other students attended college by working as they studied. So once again he took his problem to God. The solution came in the most unexpected way.

A baby, healthy and strong, arrived at the Rouse home. Elizabeth's mother longed to see her new grandson, but a heart ailment prohibited her from traveling. So she sent a ticket and asked that Elizabeth bring the baby to visit in California for a while.

But soon word came to Cliff from Elizabeth's mother telling of his wife's illness. "If you want to see Elizabeth alive again, you'd better come at once." In a short time Cliff was out on the road hitchhiking, trying to get to California as soon as possible.

The piercing cold of the mountain winter seemed to eat right through Cliff's meager clothing. Ignoring the warnings of friends, he hopped aboard a train heading west. Riding in an empty boxcar, rattling and grinding for long, numbing hours, Cliff had to jog around and around inside the car to keep from freezing.

The train was turned back by heavy snow in the Sierra passes; so he took to the highways and made a long southern detour, arriving exhausted, hungry, and cold at his destination.

With relief he found Elizabeth feeling much better and the situation much less grim than before.

A succession of events following the trip to California eventually led him into the post of foreman of a ranch in central California. As the months passed, Cliff's wages increased, and living conditions became more comfortable. Family life took a turn for the better, and Cliff thought once again about his future. Soon he arranged to take voice lessons, and this led to appointments at church services, weddings, and funerals.

Many times while working on the ranch, Cliff and Elizabeth were unable to attend worship services on Sabbath mornings, as they lived too far away. On one such morning, when they didn't feel they could make the trip, a strange shifting of circumstances altered their plans.

"Elizabeth, for some strange reason I feel compelled to go to church today." Cliff announced as he came in from milking.

"That's funny," Elizabeth replied, a puzzled look on her face. "I feel the same way."

Quickly they finished the chores, changed their clothes, and were soon on their way. When they arrived at the Palo Alto Seventh-day Adventist Church and were handed the church bulletin, they scanned the program but still found no clue as to why they felt impressed to attend church that day. Not until the speaker was introduced—a Bible teacher from Pacific Union College—did they guess the reason.

At the door of the church, Cliff asked the teacher—Elder Emmerson—if he could meet with him later in the day.

"I'm afraid we'll be late doing the milking tonight," Cliff said to Elizabeth as they waited in town for the appointed meeting time.

"Good evening, Mr. and Mrs—ah—"

"Rouse," Cliff supplied the name.

"Elder Emmerson, I'm interested in attending college; but I need to find work before I can begin. Is there anything available around the college?"

"Work is a bit of a problem," Elder Emmerson mused.

"The college is located some distance from any town or city. The St. Helena Sanitarium is about five miles from the school. Are you a nurse, Mrs. Rouse?"

"No," Elizabeth answered, "but I can do other things, such as cleaning and working in the laundry."

He directed the next question to Cliff.

"Do you know anything about horses?— Let's see, your first name is—"

"Clifford," he answered, waiting eagerly for the professor to finish his question.

"Well, Clifford, the farm manager told me

just as I was leaving on this trip that if I found a man who knew anything about horses, to send him right up."

Cliff's eyes lighted up as he glanced quickly at Elizabeth.

"I was raised on a ranch and have handled horses all my life," Cliff told him. "Right now I'm the foreman of a ranch east of here."

"Why, it seems you are just the man Professor Baldwin is looking for." Suddenly Cliff had a new job.

Before making the trip north to meet the farm manager at Pacific Union College, Cliff learned that Mr. Baldwin also raised and broke horses to sell to farmers in nearby communities. When he met the manager later, he told him of his experience in breaking horses.

"You go ahead and register and get moved up here. And as soon as you're ready, come over to the farm office, and I will give you all the work you have time for."

That evening Cliff and Elizabeth held a song of praise in their hearts as they thanked God for the amazing way He led them.

When registration day finally came, Cliff was preplexed. What course should he take? Not feeling especially gifted as a public speaker, he decided to pursue the line in which he felt most capable. Above all, he wanted to become a singing evangelist.

At that time there was no prescribed course offered in such a field; it was largely unheard of. He counseled with the instructors in the music department. Professor Noah Paulin and Miss Ivalyn Law suggested voice lessons, music directing, and sight reading.

After hearing him sing, Miss Law invited Cliff to sing in the a cappella choir. The following spring she herself enrolled for a special instructor's class at the Walker School of Music in Oakland. In the evening, after her return from the class, she tutored Cliff on the things she had learned. Cliff often went with one of the teams of theology students, who held evangelistic meetings at towns near the college. Occasionally, Elder W. R. French went along and observed them as they worked.

"Clifford, I like your singing," Elder French remarked one evening as they drove home. "You have a way of selecting songs that will win souls." On another occasion he told Cliff that if he ever needed a recommendation, to use his name as a reference. But despite repeated inquiries, no conference seemed to be interested in a singing evangelist. Theology students with musical inclinations were preferred.

Several years passed as studies and work assumed more and more of Cliff's time. During this busy period, a Bible instructor encouraged Elizabeth and Cliff to take a Bible worker's course by correspondence. She offered to act as the monitor and give them names of new interests who would welcome the young couple as they studied the Scriptures together. Soon Cliff began to conduct cottage meetings. The district pastor later sent him out on Sabbaths to preach at nearby churches.

The young couple progressed in their Christian witnessing techniques and gained the experience that only years can provide.

One day Cliff received a telegram from the president of the Central California Conference asking if he and Elizabeth would meet with him and the members of the conference committee at Modesto Union Academy. Only after the telegram was read and reread did Cliff even dare to hope that his days as a lay Bible instructor would be broadened to include conference-sponsored efforts. This meant, he knew, that he could devote his full time to the church's program of soul winning.

Of course both Cliff and Elizabeth were eager to meet this important appointment to be interviewed by members of the committee. After some minutes of deliberation, the chairman spoke earnestly to Cliff.

"Brother Rouse, we need a man to assist Brother Campbell with some meetings at Santa Maria. Are you willing to go?"

Within a few days Cliff and his little family traveled down the scenic Pacific Coast—on God's errand—to begin a life of fuller service for Him.

As Cliff stood in the pulpit, looking at the faces in his congregations—some eager, some despairing, some longing—he often recalled the rocky path he had traveled in his young manhood and how God's love had surrounded him each step of the way. To tell of this love became the work of his entire life.